A STRANGE SPELL

THE WITCH OF HENBANE ISLAND
BOOK 7

POPPY BRIDGEMAN

Ebook ISBN: 978-1-990509-73-5
Paperback ISBN: 978-1-990509-74-2

Cover created by Getcovers

FREE BOOK

Use the QR code to Claim your copy of Magic Will Out when you sign up for my newsletter and follow Cossi as she seeks answers to her past.

1

I wasn't sure if I was getting better at the advanced binding spells or if I was just becoming more comfortable looking incompetent while I practiced. Maybe both. The silvery threads of magic were weaving themselves into something that resembled the pattern Mrs. V had shown me, which felt like progress. Or at least less like complete failure than yesterday's attempt. We'd been at this for a couple of hours, and my breakfast was all used up. I needed a break and a snack.

I'd been through a lot since my discovery that I was a witch, moving to Henbane, solving a lot of murders, uncovering a decades-long lie, and learning I was one of the very few protectors of the magical world. I'm still not super sure what that means, but I'd taken a case on the mainland and done a good job—according to Destroyer, my crow familiar, and my mentor. I figured it was more about the help I got from my friends.

"Less catastrophic than your usual efforts," Mrs. V said, watching the spell settle into place. From her, it was huge praise. I'd learned that she didn't hand out compliments;

you had to dig them out of what she said, and ignore how she said it. "You've finally stopped fighting yourself."

The spell felt different this time—like my magic had stopped arguing with me about what I wanted it to do. Maybe I could trust it? Or myself, I guess. "It's still nowhere near as clean as yours."

"I've had more than a century longer than you to work out the best way," she said with a dismissive shrug. "You've had less than six months. I don't expect miracles."

From her cushion by the window, Tulip stretched and showed off her impressive lynx fangs in what might have been a yawn. At five months old, she was still very much a teenager in cat terms. Unfortunately for me, her mob boss attitude didn't mellow as she grew.

She licked her paw while still keeping eye contact with me. "Don't get cocky, I don't forgive as easily as others."

My language skill meant I understood her implied threat. "I think Destroyer will be on my side," I said, knowing Mrs. V had heard the exchange. I could only hope that his megalomania would be enough to keep Tulip in line. And he would just support me because of our link; he liked me.

"Yes," he said in my mind. "I have empire business to attend to, so please manage the cat without me."

"Tulip, play nice," Mrs. V said. She couldn't hear Destroyer, only Tulip. "You agreed to act civilized, do not let me down."

Tulip didn't blink, just stared at me as she cleaned her fur.

"Marcus seems to be doing well," I said, trying to shift the conversation to something less focused on my magical inadequacies.

"The boy's magic has stabilized now he is on Henbane,"

Mrs. V said, pouring herself another cup of tea. "Perhaps that has more to do with feeling safe than anything else. I can only imagine what would have happened in Vancouver if he'd displayed someone's romantic fantasies on the side of a building."

I laughed at the idea, but she was right. The Vancouver council was ready to send him away to a scary abandoned school to keep their community safe.

"He's learning to manage his emotions, which is good for everyone's privacy." Mrs. V settled back in her chair. "But we have bigger problems."

Every time we had one of these conversations, I felt like I was being handed a piece of a puzzle that was much bigger than I was ready to handle and maybe pieces from multiple puzzles. "Which of the larger problems?" I mean, there were so many.

"The shortage of protectors, is the root of most others." Mrs. V's expression grew more serious. "There are communities out there who think they need to handle their problems without calling us. The balance is fragile between protecting the world and the individual."

My stomach did that familiar little flip it did whenever Mrs. V reminded me that being a protector meant more than just solving problems on Henbane. The magical world was vast, and most of it was struggling along without the support system I'd grown accustomed to here. Our job was to protect the magical world, and that meant helping to solve problems. "Is it that widespread?"

"It's getting more complicated every year as the world changes." She took a sip of tea. "More protectors would help, but you can't force the calling on someone. It chooses who it chooses."

I heard the unspoken jab about whatever it was

choosing me. Well, she didn't show that in her emotions, so maybe it came from inside me. I thought about my own chaotic introduction to the protector role. How much I'd fumbled and second-guessed myself through every case before anyone knew I had those powers. And, let's face it, my job wasn't solving murders, right?

I guess I was one of the lucky ones, with Mrs. V to guide since taking over my mentorship from Phillip, who turned out to be a murdering monster. "I had everything to learn when I got here. Still do."

"I try not blame your parents for that," Mrs. V said without softening the words. "I understand the impulse, but we can't all hide as plain humans."

She was quiet for a moment, and I sensed her weighing something. Her emotions carefully shielded, as always, but I caught just a hint of concern threading through her mental barriers.

"Still," she continued, "it's been quiet around here lately. December on Henbane is usually peaceful. I suppose since Phillip is gone we can get back to normal."

I thought about Christmas—the lights everywhere, the music, the general sense of anticipation that built through the entire month, things I missed. Henbane's quieter traditions carried their own appeal. Family gatherings, reflection, simple traditions that focused more on gratitude than commerce.

"I miss shopping for presents," I admitted.

Before I could ask what people here did when they had no family, the phone rang.

Mrs. V raised an eyebrow at me. It was her phone, but I guess she wasn't in the mood to talk to anyone.

"I'll get it," I said, reaching for the phone. Maybe it would be something simple. Someone wanting to book a video session to solve a simple problem.

"Mrs. Vestum?" The woman said in German-accented English. Tension vibrated through the line even though she kept it out of her voice.

"No, I'm Cossi Fortuna. Can I help you?" I should have just handed the phone to Mrs. V, but something made me want to try handling protector business myself for once. At least I could find out what the call was about.

"We need a protector," the voice said.

"I am one. Who am I talking to?" Was there somewhere I should register so people can contact me rather than go through Mrs. V?

There was a sigh across the connection, then a resigned tone that suggested this wasn't the answer she'd been hoping for. "Grete Hoffman. I'm calling from Dresden, and I have a problem."

I grabbed a pen and paper from Mrs. V's counter. I sat

straight and told myself to look professional so that I'd sound it. "What kind of problem?"

The explanation that followed was both straightforward and completely outside my experience. A crafting spell at a Christmas market had gone rogue—something that they'd used a hundred times had hopped from the original target. The usual magical controls weren't working, and they needed it fixed before the market opened in the morning, or they'd have to close it down. The market was the community's major source of income.

It sounded complicated. More complicated than anything I'd dealt with on my own. And it was halfway around the world, in a different time zone.

I looked over at Mrs. V, who had heard enough of the conversation to understand what was happening. She was making dismissive gestures that preceded her telling me I was overthinking something.

After I'd taken down Grete's contact information and hung up, Mrs. V was quiet for a moment. She was studying me with an expression I learned was the first step in her lecturing me about my abilities.

"Well?" I asked.

"You're going," she said.

"Am I? Because that sounded like complex magical work you should handle." Why did that come out like a teenager refusing to take out the garbage?

"I'm far too old to go rushing halfway around the world to deal with someone else's botched spell," Mrs. V said with a dismissive wave. "Besides, it sounds exactly what a protector should be able to manage. And you are a protector."

Anxiety was building in my chest now. "I've never done this kind of thing. What if I can't fix it?"

"Then you'll figure out something else to try. That's what protectors do—they solve problems, they don't make excuses." Mrs. V's expression didn't soften. "Besides, you won't be completely alone. Destroyer can still communicate with you, even if he can't make the physical journey."

"Wait! Destroyer can't come with me?"

"Airlines tend to frown on crows in the passenger cabin, and cargo holds aren't suitable for any living creatures," Mrs. V said. "But your mental connection isn't limited by distance. He'll be available for consultation and confidence boosting."

I heard a tap on the patio window and saw Destroyer standing on the patio. "I am not a mere consultant! I am an emperor!"

Tulip must have relayed his speech because Mrs. V cleared her throat and stared at him. "Mark and D are both tied up on tasks for the committee. We can't risk delaying the work to solve the selfie problem."

The committee formed to address the problem of selfies and selfishness. The spell to hide the magical community, blurred the images. It was only a matter of time before someone asked an AI to figure out the problem. I couldn't justify taking any attention away from their work.

The nervous flutter in my stomach was turning into full anxiety now. Going to Germany alone to deal with magical problems I'd never encountered, working with witches I'd never met. Sure, it felt like something a real protector should be able to handle with no need to call in backup every five minutes. I still needed training. I barely knew how to solve problems on Henbane, let alone the wider world.

"All right," I said, trying to sound more confident than I felt. "I'll call Grete back and tell her I'm coming."

Mrs. V nodded. "Pack light and pack quickly. You need

to get there fast and that's going to require luck. Have Didier book your trip."

As I headed for the phone to call Grete back, Tulip's voice followed me, "Try not to embarrass the island. We have a reputation to maintain."

"A wise emperor thrives under pressure," Destroyer added from the patio.

I was going to arrive exhausted along with my fear of getting everything wrong. It would be nice if someone just said 'you'll be fine' with a bit of confidence, rather than threats and backhanded compliments; maybe I'd believe it.

3

I 'd only traveled on the local ferry until today. We'd been poor, not that I noticed as a kid, so going on holiday meant a day trip. I could only hope that the journey from Henbane to Dresden wasn't a good example of what I'd face in the future.

It was a relief that the ferry arrived as scheduled. The flights? Another story. To get from Vancouver to Dresden, I'd taken a lot of stops. The tea I brought to help me sleep was great for only one leg. I arrived in Dresden at seven in the morning, which was convenient, but it felt like someone had packed me into a bag and shaken me vigorously. By the time I stumbled off the plane at what my body insisted was the middle of the night, though the clock claimed it was early morning, every muscle ached and my brain felt wrapped in cotton. How was I supposed to solve this problem if I couldn't think?

I reached out to Destroyer as I walked to the exit and learned the downside of being halfway across the world from a crow. He was sleeping while I was awake. It was going to take a lot of coordination to get help from him if I needed it.

I spotted two people standing near the information desk, one holding a small sign with my name written in neat handwriting. Both looked to be in their sixties, but you never know with witches; they could be over a hundred or in their mid-thirties. The two bundled up against the December cold. I was glad I'd remembered to pack sweaters and my heavy coat.

"*Guten Morgen*," the woman said as I approached. Then she shook her head and switched to English. "You must be Cossi. I'm Trudi Meister, and this is Heinz Bauer. We're both on the market committee."

"Thank you for meeting me," I said, trying to project professional competence despite feeling like the only things holding me together were caffeine and stubbornness. "If it's more comfortable, please speak German. I can follow along just fine. I have to warn you, I'm not sure what I'm walking into."

"None of us are, to be honest," Heinz said with a grunt that might have been sympathy. He was stocky and solid, with calloused hands and dirt under his fingernails—an earth witch. "That's why we called for help. Car's this way."

The drive through Dresden in the pre-dawn darkness gave me glimpses of what looked like a fascinating city. Historic buildings mixed with modern reconstruction, all dusted with snow that sparkled under the streetlights. Under different circumstances—like when I wasn't half-asleep and worried about magical disasters—I might have enjoyed the scenery.

"The *Striezelmarkt* has been running for nearly six hundred years," Trudi said from the front passenger seat. "It's one of Germany's oldest Christmas markets. Our village and the entire magical community in the area depends on the income it generates."

"And now we might have to close early because of one witch's spell gone sideways," Heinz added, frustration clear. "So close to Christmas Eve. This is our biggest earning period."

I could understand their panic. A Christmas market closing unexpectedly wouldn't just be a financial disaster; it would draw unwanted attention from plain humans, the sort of scrutiny magical communities spent enormous effort avoiding—and the biggest of my responsibilities. "What exactly is happening with the spell?"

"You'll see soon enough," Trudi said.

The *Striezelmarkt*, even in the early morning, looked like Santa Claus was in residence. Wooden booths lined the square in neat rows, strings of lights casting glow over displays of crafts, food, and Christmas decorations. I pulled in the warm aroma of cinnamon and mulled wine lingered in the cold air as people prepared for the day, and I could imagine how enchanting it must be when fully operational.

Then my senses picked up a wrongness. It started as an off-tune buzz. The magical atmosphere felt jangled, discordant in a way that made my teeth ache. As we approached one particular stall, the sensation intensified until my skin was crawling with itches.

"Felix should be here by now," Heinz said, checking his watch. "We asked him to meet us early, before the other vendors arrive."

The problematic stall sold wooden toys and ornaments. Beautifully carved pieces that would have delighted any child. But something was very wrong with the magic surrounding them. The air shimmered, and I caught glimpses of light that shouldn't be there, like miniature auroras flickering around the carved figures. How long before they became visible to anyone?

"There he is," Trudi said, pointing to a man hurrying across the square.

Felix looked to be in his forties. I could sense exhaustion rolling off him in waves—not just tired, but bone-deep weary.

"Are you the protector?" he asked, looking me up and down with barely concealed doubt. "You're very young?"

"That's me," I said, ignoring the age comment. "Can you tell me what happened?"

Felix's explanation was straightforward enough. He'd cast a simple enhancement spell on his wooden toys three days ago. Something he'd done dozens of times before to make them more appealing to children. The magic was supposed to make them more attractive to touch and give children happy feelings when they played with them; nothing that would seem magical. Nothing to harm kids or make someone who couldn't afford it buy them.

Instead, the spell had fed on itself, growing stronger and more chaotic by the hour. Now the toys were radiating magical energy, and the effect was spreading to other items in nearby stalls.

"We tried standard containment," Trudi said, frustration glowing an electric blue around her. "Reversal spells, magical dampening fields, removing the affected items. Nothing worked. If anything, our interventions seemed to make it worse."

I reached out with my power, trying to understand what I was dealing with. The spell felt like an engine that had lost its controller, racing faster and faster with no way to slow down. Maybe it was linked to Felix? Spells normally wouldn't cling, but he wasn't in full health by the look of him.

"You look tired," I said. All his emotions were on display, but I could only make out the dull brown of fear and hopelessness. "Have you been getting enough sleep?"

They all looked at me with surprise. "What does that have to do with anything?" Felix asked.

"Just wondering. Sometimes when we're run down, our magic doesn't behave the way we expect it to." I wondered why they didn't know something simple like that. Were these people hiding something?

Felix's face went defensive. "I've been working hard to prepare for the Christmas season. Everyone's tired this time of year. Nothing more than usual. I'll be fine when we get back to the village and I can rest."

That was probably true, but something about the situation felt off to me. Still, I was here to fix a spell problem, not diagnose someone's sleep habits. And frankly, I wanted breakfast and about twelve hours of sleep more than I wanted to unravel complex magical mysteries.

I thought about everything I'd learned since arriving at Henbane. The hexes we'd removed floated to the top. "Let me try something," I said, approaching the stall with more confidence than I felt.

The truth was, I did not know if this was going to work. Hexes were one thing, but this wasn't a layer of evil;, it was the spell Felix cast. But I was a protector, and protectors were supposed to solve problems. And I needed to try something, right? I reached out with my protector power, not trying to understand or analyze the rogue spell, but simply asking it to stop.

The change was immediate, the chaos stabilized, the wild fluctuations smoothing out into something manageable. Shimmering lights around the wooden toys faded to their intended subtle enhancement.

For a moment, everyone just stared. I held my breath waiting for it to go back to crazy, but my order held.

"How did you do that?" Felix asked, examining his now properly enchanted toys.

"Sometimes the direct approach works better than trying to be clever about it," I said, hoping that sounded like I knew what I was doing.

Heinz picked up one of the wooden ornaments, turning it over in his weathered hands. "The enhancement is what it should be now. Perfect."

"The magical resonance is stable," Trudi added, relief clear in her voice. "Whatever you did, it worked."

"So the market can open?" I asked. "Without you closing the stall?"

"Yes," Felix said, wonder creeping into his voice as he picked up one of his wooden animals. The carved horse radiated warmth and happiness, inviting without being obviously magical. "This is what it should be. We will sell what we need to get us by."

I felt a rush of satisfaction that was way out of proportion to what I'd accomplished. Maybe Mrs. V was right; sometimes being a protector was less about having all the answers and more about being willing to try something when everyone was expecting you to perform a miracle.

As we prepared to leave the now-peaceful market, my stomach rumbled loudly enough to be embarrassing. The magical crisis was resolved. Felix's spell was working perfectly, and the *Striezelmarkt* could open. I might have almost killed myself getting here, but it was worth the effort. And now I had a short German holiday.

"There's a wonderful bakery just two streets over," Trudi

said as we walked back to their car. "They do good German breakfasts. Your magic needs feeding."

My stomach rumbled again in response, which seemed like answer enough. But as I thought about it, the whole situation felt peculiar. They'd asked me to fly halfway around the world to solve a problem that took me less than two minutes to fix. I'm not saying they didn't need a protector, but there should be one closer.

"Actually," I said, "would it make sense for me to stick around for a day or two? Make sure the spell stays stable? I mean, it seems silly to travel so far for such a quick fix."

They exchanged glances. "That's very thoughtful," Trudi said. "Though I'm sure the spell will hold. Your work seemed quite thorough."

"Still, better safe than sorry. And I've never been to a German Christmas market before." And I couldn't face getting back on another plane right now.

Felix, who had been examining his toys, looked up with more enthusiasm than I'd seen from him yet. "You should stay," he said, a spark of yellow joy clearing out the hopelessness. "The market is something special during full operation. I'd like to thank you. Maybe my partner and I could take you to breakfast?"

4

The breakfast place Trudi recommended turned out to be a cozy German cafe. Dark wood tables, checked tablecloths, and the smell of fresh bread and coffee strong enough to wake the dead greeted us as soon as we stepped inside. After the airplane coffee experience, I wasn't sure my nervous system could handle more caffeine, but I was willing to risk it.

Felix's partner Tobi turned out to be a cheerful man in his thirties who arrived at the restaurant with snow in his dark hair and a bouncing energy. He was a shifter, and like the ones on Henbane, he looked like he stepped off a magazine cover.

"So you're the miracle worker," he said. Then he settled into the chair next to Felix and hugged him, which made me think they would be together forever. "Felix has been beating himself up over that spell since it first hiccupped."

"It wasn't anything special," I said, trying not to sound too pleased with myself. "Sometimes fresh eyes help."

Felix looked better in the warm light of the restaurant, though I still noticed the tired lines around his eyes. "I've been doing enhancement spells for years," he said, stirring sugar into his coffee. "I can't understand what went wrong this time."

Tobi reached over and squeezed his hand. "You've been pushing yourself too hard lately. Working late every night, getting up early to prep for the market. Maybe your magic was just tired too."

I nodded along while wondering if this was how other magical communities worked—not knowing the basics about health and power. My inner critic voice pointed out that people were just being polite and hiding their 'duh' comments. I was too tired to fight back against that voice.

"That happens more than people think," I said. "You know how magic responds to our physical and emotional state. When we're run down, spells can get... unpredictable. Mostly weakened but sometimes weird."

"Is that your professional opinion, Dr. Fortuna?" Felix asked with a slight smile, though I could tell he was still worried about it.

"Well, I'm not a healer," I admitted with a grin. "But I've seen it happen. On Henbane, we had someone whose garden spells kept growing vegetables the wrong colors when she was stressed about her daughter's wedding."

Tobi laughed at that. "What color vegetables?"

"Bright purple carrots. Electric blue tomatoes. The aesthetic was... memorable, but thankfully, the taste wasn't affected."

That got a genuine laugh from Felix, which lifted his exhaustion, making him appear ten years younger. "At least my toys didn't turn purple."

We spent a pleasant hour eating what they assured me was a regular breakfast: fresh rolls with butter and jam, soft-boiled eggs, sliced meats and cheeses, and coffee that lived up to its promising aroma. Tobi kept the conversation light, asking about Henbane and my experiences as someone who lived as a plain human. Felix gradually relaxed and started looking more like he wasn't carrying the weight of the world on his shoulders.

I kept sensing the undercurrents despite the outward fun. Felix's emotions remained muted. When he laughed at Tobi's stories about problematic customers at the store, there was an underlying thread of anxiety that never quite faded—a low hum of acid green tension that threaded through everything he was feeling.

I couldn't let go of the thought that there was something behind the tiredness. Maybe something my protector power was trying to point out. "You know," I said as we finished breakfast, "it might not be a bad idea to have someone take a look at you. Just to make sure everything's okay."

Tobi and Felix exchanged glances. "Grete Hoffman has been treating him for some persistent fatigue," Tobi said. "That's how she knew to call for help. When the spell went wrong, she thought there might be something she missed."

She could have mentioned it on the phone. "And what does she think is causing the fatigue?"

"Nothing definitive yet," Felix said, clearly uncomfortable with the topic. "Just stress and overwork."

He was hiding something, but pressing the issue didn't seem like the right approach. "Well, you know your situation better than I do. Just... don't ignore it if it gets worse, okay?"

As we finished up the last morsels of our meal, I felt refreshed enough to ask about what I should do while I was in Dresden.

"Would you like a tour of the market?" Tobi offered. "It's something to see when it's bustling with families."

I was about to accept when my phone rang. The international number looked familiar. Mrs. V calling from Henbane. "I should take this," I said as an apology, then stepped outside into the crisp December air.

"You arrived," she said. "You could have sent a text."

"Sorry, I guess I was focusing on my job," I said. I felt guilty for not thinking about her. "The problem is fixed, by the way. Took about ten minutes including talking about it. The spell just needed a firm hand."

"Ten minutes." Her tone was flat. "I suppose that's better than your usual fumbling around for hours. I stayed up late for good reason then."

"Yes, no need for you to lose sleep," I said, trying not to sound resentful that I'd lost a ton of sleep. Then again, I was twenty-one, and she was probably a hundred and fifty. I would recover faster.

"And the witch who cast it?" she asked.

"Felix? He seems okay. Tired, maybe a little run down, but nothing dramatic. Why?"

There was a pause that carried Mrs. V's particular brand of disapproval. "Something about this whole situation doesn't sit right with me."

My body tensed. Mrs. V's instincts about magical situations were spot on, and she wasn't the only one. This must be why I was so pushy about Felix seeing a healer.

"What kind of doesn't sit right?" I asked, not willing to share my doubts first.

"I don't know precisely," she said. "Shutting down an erratic spell shouldn't need a protector. With so few of us, we need to be efficient."

I looked through the restaurant window at Felix and Tobi, who were chatting over the remains of their breakfast.

They seemed like a typical couple enjoying their morning. Nothing dramatic or mysterious about them.

"Maybe it's just because I solved the problem so quickly?" I suggested. "It feels anticlimactic?"

"Maybe," Mrs. V said, but she didn't sound convinced. "You decided to stay a few days, didn't you?"

"Yes, that seemed like the sensible thing to do. Get to know the local magical community, make sure the spell holds. Try to figure out what's going on," I said. "And if another crisis comes up in Europe, I'm here."

"Good. Trust your instincts on this one," she said, sounding as if she was proud of me. "If it's telling you to look deeper, do it."

That was a big ask. I was still pretty new at this protector business, and the difference between genuine intuition and paranoia isn't always clear to me. I promised to keep her updated and ended the call.

When I went back inside, Felix and Tobi were getting ready to leave. "Everything all right?" Tobi asked, noting my expression.

"Mrs. V agrees I should stick around for a bit," I said. "Make sure everything's settled."

"That's not a bad idea. We don't want to burn out our protectors," Felix said. "And we'd love to show you around. Grete would like to meet you too. She's been looking into some ancient theories about health and power."

I'd never had much opportunity to discuss theory. I wasn't a healer, but a protector needed to cover all the specialties, at least a bit. Doc Rene on Henbane was more a figure it out and fix it kind of healer.

"Plus," Felix added with more enthusiasm than I'd heard from him all morning, "Christmas season in Dresden is special. Other markets have different products, the atmosphere is so invigorating, the traditional celebrations are lively. You should think of your stay as a holiday, yes?"

The idea of going from event to event right now over-whelmed me. I need to recharge first. "Thank you for the offer of a tour," I said. "But, after all that traveling, I think I need some sleep to fully enjoy the experience. I'm happy to wander around on my own for a bit, get my bearings."

"Of course," Tobi said. "The market's easy enough to navigate. Just follow the crowds and the smell of roasted chestnuts."

My mouth watered at the thought of the treats available. How was I still hungry? "I'll need to find a hotel, and I should get my bag back from Trudi."

"Already taken care of," Tobi said with a grin. "I called ahead while you were on the phone and arranged for a hotel room. And Trudi said she'd drop your bag off there this afternoon. It's a lovely place not far from the market."

5

After checking in and taking a much-needed nap, I cleaned up and headed out to explore. Dresden in December was beautiful. Snow dusted the baroque architecture, lights twinkled in shop windows, and there was a sense of anticipation in the air that had nothing to do with magic and everything to do with tradition. I took a deep breath and started walking.

The *Striezelmarkt* was a mix of magical and mundane vendors, plain humans selling traditional foods and toys alongside witches whose stalls carried that extra something that made everything seem more festive. I could sense the enchantments woven through the magical booths; warming spells to keep the mulled wine at the perfect temperature, preservation charms on the fresh bread, and happiness enchantments so subtle they felt like natural good cheer rather than magical enhancement.

Tourists, both plain and magical, wandered through as though there was nothing unusual. I was fascinated by how seamlessly the two worlds blended together, though no one appeared to notice the power flowing. A plain human buying hand-carved ornaments from a witch's stall. A witch couple deciding between two different artisan breads from a plain human's selection.

By the afternoon, I was wandering through the reconstructed old town when I spotted a woman with silver-streaked brown hair examining something in her hands. As I got closer, I saw it was a small pouch that gave off a faint herbal scent of medicinal magic. I could hear her speaking to someone on the phone, and I recognized the voice.

"Excuse me," I said as I approached. "Are you Grete Hoffman?"

She looked up in surprise. "Yes, and you must be Cossi. Felix described you quite well. Thank you for coming so quickly."

"Nice to meet you in person," I said. "I appreciate the time to visit such a lovely city."

She smiled at that, though I caught a blush of deep blue worry in her emotions that didn't quite match her expression. "Walk with me? I was hoping to have a chance to speak with you while you're here."

We strolled along the Elbe River, past tourists taking photos of the historic skyline. The late afternoon light cast everything in golden tones, which made the snow appear dusted with glitter.

"Have you checked on Felix since this morning?" I asked.

"He's feeling better, I think. The spell resolution seems to have lifted a weight off his shoulders. But..." She paused, choosing her words. "I'm still concerned about the underlying issues."

Was this what Mrs. V and I sensed? "What kind of underlying issues?"

Grete was quiet for a moment, and I sensed her wrestling with something. "I wanted to discuss with you. As a protector, you might have insights I'm missing. His condition is not responding to the usual treatments"

"I'm happy to help if I can." I had no idea what I could do beyond listening.

She struggled with what to tell me. I wondered if she was about to violate some oath. "It's not just that his exhaustion is persistent. Some symptoms are... unusual for simple overwork or stress."

"I don't know enough to understand that," I said. "What specifically is different?"

"In my experience, exhaustion presents in predictable patterns. The person's power reserves deplete gradually. They need more rest between casting. That sort of thing. But Felix's magic seems to fluctuate wildly, sometimes stronger than normal, sometimes barely there at all."

I thought about the rogue spell, how it had felt like an engine without a governor. "Could that be what caused the enhancement spell to go wrong?"

"That's my theory. But I can't figure out what's causing the fluctuations." Grete stopped walking and turned to face me. "Have you ever seen anything like this before?"

"This is my second assignment," I said, trying not to sound like I was making an excuse. "I've studied all kinds of tings, but no, I haven't. Could it be external? Something affecting his magic from outside?"

"That's what I keep coming back to," Grete said with a shrug. "But I can't detect any foreign magical influences, no curses or hexes or ongoing spells that might be interfering."

She had a point about different areas of expertise. Healers focused on medical issues, while protectors dealt with... well, with people who caused problems for magical communities. The overlap wasn't always obvious.

"Would you like me to take a look?" I asked. "I can't diagnose medical issues, but I come at it from a different angle."

"Thank you, I was hoping you'd offer," Grete said with obvious relief. "Felix is planning to work the market again tomorrow, and then we're all heading up to the village for Christmas. Would you be interested in joining us? For the week?"

My power surged and then ebbed to the normal background level. Even if I didn't want to hang around, I couldn't ignore the hint. "Where is the village?"

"About an hour south of here, up in the mountains. It's not like Henbane, but we're isolated, and only witches and shifters live there or can visit. We always spend Christmas there together, like a big extended family."

"That sounds wonderful," I said. "Are you sure I wouldn't be intruding?"

"Not at all. We love having visitors, especially witches from other parts of the world. And..." she hesitated, then continued, "having a protector around might not be a bad idea."

"To observe Felix, or is something else going on?"

"Nothing dramatic. Just... well, you'll see when you get there. We've got some powerful personalities on the council, and they don't always agree on how things should be handled. Sometimes an outside perspective helps keep things civil."

That sounded familiar. Every magical community I'd encountered, in person or on video, seemed to have at least one or two people who thought their way was the only way to do things.

"I'd love to come," I said. "Though I should warn you, I don't know anything about traditional German Christmas celebrations."

"Don't worry about that. We'll teach you everything you need to know." Grete said.

The next morning, I met Felix, Tobi, and Grete at the market square. The *Striezelmarkt* had closed for the season the night before, and the vendors were finishing the last of their packing.

Felix looked better than he had when I first met him—less tired, more present—but I could still sense those underlying currents of anxiety and exhaustion that seemed to cling to him.

"Ready for a real German Christmas?" Tobi asked with a grin as we loaded our bags into Grete's car.

"As ready as I can be," I said.

The drive south from Dresden was beautiful, taking us through snow-covered countryside and into foothills that became mountains. The higher we climbed, the more I could sense the similarities with home. Isolated, and somehow generating a feeling of safety.

"There," Grete said, pointing ahead to where the road seemed to dead-end at a wall of forest. "Can you feel it?"

There was a concealment spell wrapped around the area ahead of us, strong and sophisticated. Something that had been there for centuries. It wasn't just hiding the village from plain human eyes. It was discouraging them from even wanting to look in this direction.

"Impressive," I said. "Henbane is kept invisible by a ward, but it's nothing like yours."

"The crossroads spell has been maintained by the village for over four hundred years," Felix said with obvious pride. "Every generation adds a little something to it."

As we approached what looked like a dead end, the concealment spell recognized us - or rather, recognized that we belonged to the magical community it protected. The forest seemed to shift, and suddenly there was a narrow road leading up into the mountains.

"Welcome to *Sicherheim*," Grete said as we climbed the winding road. "Population two hundred seventy-six, and almost every one of us a witch."

"Almost?" I asked.

"We have one shifter," she said with a glance at Tobi in the rearview mirror. "But it's a witch community that's been here for centuries."

The village, when it came into view, was exactly what I'd imagined a German village would look like. Stone houses with steep roofs clustered around a small square, smoke rising from chimneys, and a cozy, lived-in atmosphere that spoke of families who'd known each other for generations.

"It's beautiful," I said, meaning it.

"Wait until you see it decorated for Christmas," Tobi said. "We decorate tonight, it's quite the village event."

6

I woke up the morning before Christmas Eve feeling more rested than I had since leaving Henbane. The little guest room in the house where Grete had set me up was cozy in the way only old mountain homes could be —thick stone walls, a comfortable bed with warm quilts, and windows that looked out over snow-covered pine forests that stretched all the way to the horizon.

I'd set my phone to wake me early enough to talk to Destroyer before he's be asleep—I hope. Six AM here meant nine PM on Henbane. Since I usually didn't have to worry about time zones, I wasn't sure what time he actually went to bed. The only thing I was sure of was that a crow couldn't mess around with their rest schedule like a human could.

"Finally," Destroyer snapped in my head as I called to him. "I require sleep to be the emperor, so let's make this fast."

For all his snappiness, I could feel his relief at my call. "Sorry. I don't have much of an update."

"No progress on this mysterious unfinished business?"

he did that kind of half-caw I'd come to recognize and his version of 'hmm'.

"No," I said. I tried to think what I could say to make this worth his lost sleep. I admit I reached out mostly to hear him talk. I guess I was lonely.

"I have no doubt that as my familiar, you will determine the problem and solve it elegantly," he said. "Tulip has suggested you are not up to the task, but I believe in you."

Wow, that lynx really didn't like me. Fine, I didn't much care for her. "I'll try to keep my contact with you to the evenings here."

"I would prefer you not to travel in the future."

"I don't get to choose," I said before wishing him a good night. Although filling up our ranks might help me stay closer to him.

I got dressed and crept downstairs, thinking I might explore the village a bit before everyone else was up—breakfast could wait. I might check in on Felix, see if his recovery was holding.

Sicherheim in the early morning was even more enchanting than it had been the night before. Fresh snow had fallen while I slept, coating everything in pristine white, and the air was so crisp and clean it almost hurt to breathe. I'd need much warmer clothes if I stayed longer. For now, a warming spell would take care of my personal temperature.

The village was laid out around a central square with a fountain that had been turned down to a trickle for winter —easier than keeping up a spell to stop the pipes freezing. Stone houses lined narrow streets that wound up the mountainside, and I could see gardens behind that must bloom beautifully in spring and summer. Everything felt settled and peaceful—a lot like Henbane.

I was wandering down a path that led toward a cluster of

trees. The local wildlife—what wasn't hibernating anyway —were hurrying around collecting nesting material and the final bits of food. A red squirrel chittered at me from a pine tree, its bushy tail twitching with curiosity. This was my opportunity to do a little snooping. Squirrels were experts at gossip.

"Good morning," I said to the squirrel.

The squirrel's head tilted, and I could sense its surprise at being addressed directly. Probably no language witches around here. "Stranger witch," it chattered, tail flicking. "Why do you speak to me?"

"I speak to animals," I said. "I wonder if you've noticed anything odd around here."

The squirrel considered this, head cocked to one side. "Mostly quiet. Good nuts, warm nests."

Of course, she thought first of her family and needs. "What about the village? The witches?"

"They don't change. You mean the dead one?"

"A dead witch? Here?"

"Yesterday. Favorite tree, too. We stay away until the body goes."

This was the reason I came. Even I couldn't doubt that this death was important. Losing a witch anytime was awful, but just before Christmas? That tainted every year going forward. I'd be the protector who found the body—not the reputation I wanted. Nothing I could do to avoid it. "Can you show me where?"

The squirrel bounded from branch to branch, leading me deeper into the small forest. I caught glimpses of others. A fox in a bush looked up. Another squirrel skittered up the trunk of a tree. A badger lumbered across my path. I wondered at the number of them out in the cold.

"There," the squirrel said, stopping at the edge of a small

clearing. In the center was a massive oak tree. "Under the big tree." She twitched her tail and then left. I guess dealing with this was better payment than a handful of seeds.

Even from a distance, the area around the oak felt wrong, unsettled in a way that made my teeth ache. The disorder of the power reminded me of the spell in Felix's stall. The dead witch was slumped against the tree, head fallen forward on his chest.

I stepped closer, and then came to a sudden stop. It was Felix. His eyes were closed, his expression peaceful, and if it hadn't been for the absolute stillness and the magical wrongness that surrounded the area, I might have thought he was just sleeping.

But he wasn't sleeping.

I kneeled down next to him, touching nothing, reaching out with my senses to understand what had happened. The magical traces around the area were chaotic—not the clean patterns I expected from a natural death—although I had less experience with that than with murder.

"Felix?" I called softly, even though I knew there wouldn't be an answer.

The surrounding forest was quiet—no birdsong, no rustle of small animals, just the absolute stillness that comes after something terrible has happened.

I sat back on my heels and tried to think. Felix was dead, and given the magical disturbance I could sense around the area, it wasn't a heart attack, or something equally natural. Which meant I was looking at a murder in a hidden magical village where everyone knew everyone else.

This was not how I'd expected to spend Christmas.

I told myself to stop stalling. The first thing I needed to do was make sure nobody else disturbed the scene. The second thing was to get help. Grete or a cop, someone who knew how to handle this kind of situation. And the third thing was to figure out how I was going to tell Tobi that his partner was dead.

I pulled out my phone to call Grete. She'd know who the local authorities were, and I needed a healer to check him, anyway.

7

I t didn't take long for Grete to arrive, and she brought help in the form of a woman I hadn't met yet— someone with a competent, no-nonsense presence that suggested she was used to handling problems. Both of them bundled up against the cold, their breath making small clouds in the mountain air as they hurried down the forest path.

"This is Klara Richter," Grete said by way of introduction as they approached. "She's our village police officer."

I wasn't entirely sure what I'd been expecting from a police officer here, but Klara looked reassuringly normal. Dark hair pulled back in a ponytail, sensible winter boots, and a jacket that had seen plenty of use. Her expression was alert and professional.

"You're the protector," Klara said, and it wasn't quite a question. "Grete told me you found a body."

"I did. About twenty minutes ago." I gestured toward Felix without getting too close. "I haven't touched anything, and I've kept everyone away from the area."

Klara nodded and pulled out a small notebook. Mark

didn't use one normally, but I guess here she might need to be more like a plain human cop. She approached Felix, examining the scene, disturbing nothing, while Grete hung back with me. Her emotions were a swirl of sadness and curiosity.

"How does he look to you?" I asked Grete.

"Peaceful," she said, her voice heavy with sadness. "Like he just... went to sleep. You said the power around here was jumpy, right? I think that means he didn't just pass on."

Klara straightened up and turned back to us. "No obvious signs of violence. No wounds, no indication of a struggle. But there's definitely something not quite right. I'm not used to dealing with this kind of crime, so I might not know what to look for."

"You can sense the power, too?" I asked, curious.

"I'm a witch. I may not have the usual police powers, but I can still sense when something's off," Klara said. "This entire area has an unsettled feeling that doesn't match someone just dying peacefully."

She lacked the normal police powers? As far as I knew, that was the ability to tell if people were lying, nothing else. Mark's ability to find things only helps when we know what we're looking for. And his third power, shielding, wasn't all that special since most witches could cast a spell to do that.

"I have some experience," I said. "I can help."

"Do you know what killed him?" Klara asked.

"No, but Grete can probably do that," I said, trying not to take her question as a knock to my value. "I've investigated several murders. There really isn't one way to go ahead with the investigation. We need information."

"Regardless of solving this, and we don't know if it's a murder," Grete said. "We'll need to notify the council. And someone has to tell Tobi."

My heart sank at that. "I can talk to Tobi if you want. I was there when they talked about Felix's health issues. He might have questions about whether this was related."

"We don't know," Grete said. "We won't have answers to his questions. He's going to be devastated."

"Before we do anything else," Klara said, flipping through her notebook, "I guess I should get your advice, Cossi. What am I missing? Is this an accident?"

"With the power doing weird things, I think it's murder," I said without hesitation. "But I can't tell why right now, or if it was just an accident."

Klara and Grete exchanged glances. "I'll take your help," Klara said. "Until we know more. I mean, we haven't had a suspicious death in the village in... well, ever, as far as I know and then you show up..."

"You called me," I said. "Do you think a protector could kill someone?"

Klara gave a low chuckle. "Just checking. No. I guess I know two people who didn't commit this crime. You because of your position, and me because I know me."

"Hey, I'm a healer," Grete said. "I can't do harm."

"Okay, three people," Klara said. "Look, we're autonomous here. We handle our own problems, our own justice. But we've never had to handle anything like this. I usually deal with kids getting up to antics."

"We'll need to secure the scene, notify the council, and start investigating," I said, trying to sound more confident than I felt. "The good news is that in a community this small, the killer is probably someone we can identify and question."

"The bad news," Grete said, "is that the killer is someone we know and trust."

That was the heart of it. In a hidden community of fewer

than three hundred people, everyone knew everyone else. Families had been neighbors for generations, children grew up together, and secrets were hard to keep. That one of them had killed Felix was going to shatter the community's sense of safety and trust.

"I agree we should call a meeting of the village council," I said. "They need to know what's happened, and we need to decide how to handle the investigation."

"The council meets in the town hall," Klara said. "I can gather them - they'll want to hear this from you directly."

"What about the body?" Grete asked.

"We'll need to move him somewhere more appropriate than the forest floor," I said. "But carefully, and after documenting everything we can about the scene first."

"I can handle that part," Grete said. "I've had medical training, even if this isn't a normal medical situation. I'll take pictures and send them to you."

As we made our plans, I thought about the animal witnesses I'd spoken with earlier. They'd known something was wrong before any of us had suspected it. That gave me an idea of where to start the investigation.

"I talked to a squirrel earlier," I said. "That's how I found out about Felix."

"That's a handy power," Klara said. "I'm not sure how we can rely on a squirrel, but the animals are everywhere."

"I understand every language," I said. "It's been the most useful one yet. I'll see if there's more to learn later."

"I wish I had that ability," Klara said. "Mine are less useful in this situation."

I didn't ask her what powers she had. It felt intrusive, and if the community trusted her ability, I would do the same.

"We'll need to be careful about how we handle this," I

said as Klara walked with me back to the village. "News of Felix's death is going to spread quickly in a community this size, and we need to make sure we get accurate information before rumors start."

"I can already imagine the crazy theories," Klara said. "We need to make sure the investigation is handled properly. I don't want people to challenge our results."

That had never occurred to me. I might need to stay aware of the fact that these people didn't have a reason to trust me beyond my title. "So far, I've been able to prove we got the right person. And mostly they've been a trusted part of their community."

The peaceful fairy tale village I'd admired yesterday was about to become a crime scene, and Christmas was going to be overshadowed by questions about who among them was a killer.

8

The hardest part of telling Tobi about Felix was watching his face as he processed the news. I'd found him in their cottage, puttering around the kitchen and humming quietly to himself. Clearly expecting Felix to come back from his morning walk with stories about the forest animals or ideas for new wood carvings.

When I explained what had happened, Tobi went still. Then he sat down heavily at their kitchen table and just stared at his hands for several long minutes.

"I knew something was wrong," he said, his voice barely above a whisper. "The last few months, he kept saying he was fine, but I could smell the exhaustion on him. He always thought he could hide things from me, but I'm a shifter. It's hard to turn off my senses."

"Grete is going to examine him," I said gently. "I promise you we'll find out what happened."

"What do you mean?" Tobi asked. "He didn't just succumb to whatever was draining him? I know witches generally know when they are about to die, but he was ill."

I hesitated. I didn't like telling him bad news, but we also didn't have many answers. This is exactly why I hated being cut off from Henbane by stupid time zones. It was all down to my judgment, and I didn't trust it at all. Regardless, I couldn't leave him without something to hold onto. "We don't know yet. But there were some... weirdness around his body."

Tobi tried to take a deep breath, but it broke into a sob. "Someone did this to him? How do you know? Who would have. Everyone loved him."

"I'll get you answers. I promise." We talked for a while longer, with Tobi providing a timeline of Felix's activities over the last few days and sharing his observations about Felix's declining health. By the time I left their cottage, I had a clearer picture of Felix's final weeks—and more questions than answers.

The village council meeting was scheduled for that afternoon, which gave me a few hours to think through what I knew and what I needed to find out. I decided to call home for advice, even though I knew it would be late on Henbane. If I couldn't talk to my familiar, I could certainly talk to my friends—and Mrs. V.

She answered on the second ring, and her voice sounded more alert than I'd expected. "Well? Have you found the real problem?"

"It's not great news, but I hope this is the reason I needed to stay," I admitted. "Felix is dead. I found his body this morning. I'm almost certain he was murdered."

"Why do you think that?" she asked. "Not every death you encounter is murder."

Way to boost my confidence. "The local police officer thinks so, and there was something wrong around him. I couldn't tell what it was."

She humphed. "I wasn't questioning your competence.

You really need to get over that. Are you handling the investigation?"

"With the local officer, yes. Her name is Klara, and she seems competent, but she mentioned she doesn't have the usual police powers. This is her first murder case, too." I thought about why that bothered me. Plain humans trained their police, so why did we rely on random magical powers? "She seems to be willing to work with me."

"Don't overthink it. Not everyone has the right powers for the job," Mrs. V said. "Communities work with whoever's available. Henbane was lucky that Mark was born with the ability to detect lies."

"When we figure out who killed him, I'm supposed to present the evidence to the council and work with them on how to proceed." A flash of the Vancouver council's ideas of handling things hit me.

"It is not your job to allow local rules to apply if you feel they are wrong," Mrs. V said. "You've already worked with one council that didn't want to balance the two sides of justice. I think we've lost track of how bad this is. A council need to serve justice that protects the community from discovery and protects the individual witches."

Easy for her to say. She wasn't alone in the mountains with a murderer on the loose. One everyone knew. "I'll remember that," I said, trying to sound like it meant something.

"This is part of a much bigger problem." She paused, and I could almost hear her picking through the right words. "We have never imposed strict rules across the magical world. It wouldn't work, each community faces different challenges. Sometimes what they think is best is protecting the community's reputation rather than pursuing justice."

Again, I'd love to hear something to build my confidence, not overwhelm it. "So what do I do? I can't just steamroll the council."

"Trust your instincts," she said, like it was that easy. "Maybe this is not the time to fight this battle. We need more... more information, more protectors, more time."

"I should go," I said. "The village is meeting and I have to figure out what to say."

She actually told me I could do what was needed. No details, of course, but a compliment. I'd have to figure this one out on my own, though I wished I had my friends there to bounce ideas off. Most of my previous investigations had involved working behind the scenes with Lilibeth, Lance, and D, and their different perspectives had always been helpful.

The village hall was older than some of the cottages, built of the same gray stone, but it had been designed as a civic building rather than being a converted house. Inside, I faced five people arranged around a large wooden table. I recognized Heinz and Trudi from my arrival in Dresden, but the other three were new to me. So, not the village, just the council.

"Cossi Fortuna," said a man who looked like he was in his sixties, with gray hair and a dignified bearing. "I'm Matthias Vogel, senior council member. Please, sit down."

The other introductions followed. Erik Brandt was younger than the others, maybe in his forties, with a restless energy. Anneliese Weber was a woman in her fifties with an unsettling directness to her gaze that made me think she saw more than I wanted her to.

"Klara tells us we have a situation," Matthias said once everyone was settled. "She briefed us on the basic situation, but we'd like to hear your assessment. As the protector, you must understand this is a threat to our safety."

I outlined what I'd found that morning—Felix's body, the magical disturbances around the area, and my conclusion that we were probably looking at murder rather than natural death.

"Such violence," Erik said, shaking his head. "In *Sicherheim*. It's hard to believe."

"Hard to believe, but perhaps inevitable," Anneliese said.

Erik looked at her. I saw a spike of violet shock. "You suspected this would happen? Why did you keep this secret?"

She rolled her eyes—a very weird look on a woman her age. "Not everything is a vision. We are human. We are isolated, eventually someone is bound to get angry enough to kill."

I hated to think she was right, but plain human history backed her up. The fact that the murder happened when I arrived wasn't great, either. "What's the normal procedure for this situation?" I asked, hoping I'd hear they had a prison somewhere just like Henbane.

"We don't have one," Matthias admitted, and I believed him. He radiated a pale yellow I interpreted as dismay, whether it was about the murder happening, or about not having a solution, I couldn't tell. "Our usual approach to serious problems is to handle them as a community, but murder..."

"Murder requires a different approach," Trudi said firmly. Her emotions were solid colors. She wasn't uncertain about anything. "We need to cooperate with the investigation and let the evidence lead where it will. We will decide on the punishment when we have our answers."

"Within reason," Erik said, and I caught not just defensiveness in his tone but a deeper current of anxiety. "We also need to consider what's best for the community as a whole."

There it was—the tension Mrs. V had warned me about. "I understand your concern for the community," I said. "But I need to be clear about my role here. As a protector, my responsibility is to find the truth about what happened to Felix, regardless of how inconvenient that truth might be."

Matthias nodded. "We appreciate that position. But we hope you'll also understand that we have to consider the broader implications. *Sicherheim* has maintained its independence and security for four centuries. We can't let that be threatened."

"I'm not here to threaten your community," I said. "But I also can't promise that the investigation won't turn up things some people would prefer to keep private."

The five council members exchanged glances, and I could sense the complex web of emotions that connected them—loyalty tinged with worry, protective instincts mixed with fear. They wanted justice for Felix, but they also wanted to protect the village they'd spent their lives maintaining.

"We'll cooperate with your investigation," Matthias said, though his emotions carried a shadow of reluctance. "But we ask that you be sensitive to our situation. Many of us have known each other for decades. Whatever happened to Felix, it's going to tear the community apart."

"I'll be as sensitive as possible while still doing my job," I said, standing up to show the meeting was over. Like I had everything under control.

Walking back through the village in the late afternoon light, I noticed how the Christmas decorations from the night before had transformed the peaceful scene. Garlands draped between the stone houses, wreaths on doors, and small lights twinkling in windows—all of it creating a festive atmosphere that felt surreal given what had happened that morning. Children were building snowmen in front of their homes, smoke rose from chimneys, and the entire scene had a cozy, timeless quality that made you forget about the outside world. It was hard to believe that somewhere in this decorated, idyllic setting, someone had committed murder.

9

The next morning, I met Klara at the village hall to plan our investigation strategy. She'd spent the evening thinking through the case, and had several pages of notes organized in neat columns that made me think of police shows I'd devoured when I lived on the mainland.

"I've been considering our approach," she said as we settled at a table with coffee and fresh pastries that smelled like heaven. "We should start with formal interviews of anyone who had regular contact with Felix. Work through them systematically."

Not exactly a new approach, but I didn't tell her that. I mean, she had it right. My previous investigations all started this way, and the breakthrough moments had come from following hunches. I was smart enough to know the hunches hadn't come out of thin air. I liked that Klara wasn't intimidated by the task. Maybe I could catch some of her confidence.

"That makes sense," I said. "Though, let's not make

everything so formal to start. If we can get people talking before they have time to think too hard about their answers, we'll learn a lot."

Klara looked skeptical. "In my experience, formal interviews yield more reliable information. People take it seriously when they know it's official."

I could understand her perspective, but I also knew she hadn't dealt with anything like this before. Instead of pointing that out, I tried a different approach.

"The thing is, as a protector, I sometimes notice things that... well, that might not show up in formal interviews." I wasn't sure how to explain this without getting into the whole emotion-reading situation, which seemed like something that should stay private for now. "I pick up on tensions between people, undercurrents, that sort of thing. But it works better when people aren't being careful about what they say. Or locked down into a position."

"Like reading micro expressions?" Klara asked, and I caught the faint skepticism in her voice. "Don't be so surprised, we aren't living in the middle ages. I guess I see your point."

"Something like that." It wasn't entirely a lie. "Would it be possible for me to spend some time just... observing? Talking to people casually? I promise I'll share anything useful I learn."

Klara considered this, tapping her pen against her notebook. I could sense her reluctance—she wanted to maintain control of the investigation, establish her authority. But she also knew she was out of her depth. Her emotions were a nauseating mix of acid green and neon purple.

"I suppose that could be helpful," she said. "Background information before we do formal statements. But I want regular updates. And don't interview anyone officially without me there. And you don't have a lot of time. Christmas is important here. We can't taint it with our investigation."

"Agreed," I said, keeping my thought that the murder had already done that damage to myself. "I was thinking I'd start by getting a feel for the village, see who's willing to talk. Maybe revisit the crime scene area too. Can you point me in the right direction?"

After Klara left, I headed back to the tree where I'd found Felix's body. The area was marked off, though there wasn't much to see in daylight that I hadn't noticed yesterday. What I needed was information that only the local animals could provide. I mean, I hadn't exactly limited my casual chatting to humans, had I?

I found the red squirrel who'd led me to Felix perched in the same pine tree and looking considerably less agitated than it had the day before.

"Good morning," I said. "I wanted to ask you more about what you and the others saw."

The squirrel's tail twitched with interest. "We know who you are now. Give food for true stories."

What the heck? "How do you know that. And I'm sorry I didn't bring food this time. I'll get some later and leave it here."

"Bird tell bird. Fly far. Tell next bird until tell us." Her tail twitched. "Eagles say not eat us for a while. Crow king tell not to."

Great. Destroyer didn't need to leave Henbane to take over the world. We're doomed. "Can you tell me anything that will help find this killer?"

"Sick human came lots of times to forest," the squirrel chattered. "Always tired, always sad. Animals smell sickness on him—not wolf-sick or bird-sick, but magic-wrong-sick."

That matched what Grete had told me about Felix's condition. "Did you see him with anyone else? Other humans?"

"Sometimes. Shifter-smell human comes with him, gentle-speaks to him. Good human." That would be Tobi. "Other humans sometimes."

I tried to think of more specific questions. Animals were excellent witnesses in some ways—their senses picked up details humans missed—but they didn't always understand the significance of what they observed. "The day Felix died, did you see or smell anything unusual?"

The squirrel considered this, head cocked thoughtfully. "Morning smells normal. Sick human comes alone, walks slow to big tree. Sits down, looks very tired. Then..." It paused, tail flicking with agitation. "Then wrong-smell comes. Not forest smell. Not usual human smell. Sharp-bitter smell that makes small animals run away."

"Sharp-bitter smell?" That could be important. "Can you describe it more?"

"Like when humans make bitter-water that burns. But with fear-smell and anger-smell from humans. Made us not want to be near."

I wasn't sure what bitter-water meant—maybe alcohol? —but the fear and anger smells were concerning. "Did you see the human who brought that smell?"

"No, only smell. Then sick human stops moving, and wrong-smell goes away. All very quiet after."

Maybe I was getting good at solving murders, which was a weird thing to be pleased about. The squirrel was describing what sounded like someone approaching Felix while he rested under the tree—someone whose emotional state had been strong enough for animals to detect even if Felix himself hadn't sensed the danger.

I spent another hour talking to various forest creatures —ravens, a few more squirrels, and a cautious fox who finally emerged from the underbrush to share what it had observed. They all told basically the same story: Felix had been getting sicker over the past few weeks, he'd come to the forest alone that morning, and sometime after he'd settled under the oak tree, someone with a very distinctive scent had come near.

"Could you identify the scent if you smell it again?" I asked the fox, who seemed the most willing to try to help.

The fox sat and tipped her head to the side. "Yes, but not for long. Humans change their smell all the time. Maybe two suns."

That gave me an idea. If I could arrange for the fox to encounter the people who'd been in contact with Felix recently, it might be able to identify who had approached him that morning. "Would you be willing to help with that?" I asked.

She considered this, golden eyes calculating. "What payment do you offer?"

Of course it would want payment—I always brought treats for the Henbane animals when I needed their help. I'd promised the squirrel some seeds. "What would you like?"

"Eggs. Two eggs for one human-sniffing." She focused on my eyes, and I felt what a hen might feel just before the attack.

"I'll see what I can arrange," I promised. Surely, a couple of eggs would be easy to get.

She refused to wander the village with me and sniff people. I'd pick up the scent by talking to suspects—that left anyone I'd talked to today off the suspect list. The upside was the case might close in a few hours. The downside? I would need to convince the council to take my word about the fox's testimony?

Or Klara, for that matter. She needed to believe in the plan so I could move forward. Something told me she was going to find my approach a little unconventional.

10

B y afternoon, I still had learned little beyond what the animals had told me. I'd wandered through the village, chatting casually with people I encountered, but everyone seemed determined to keep conversations focused on Christmas Eve preparations rather than Felix's death.

It's hard to keep confidence up when you have no leads, and it's Christmas. I was supposed to be with my new family, not alone in a foreign country, stuck in the mountains. I decided to try thinking about something else for a while— you know, stop worrying about the problem and let your mind figure it out.

I ducked into the village bakery for a late lunch—more of those incredible pastries and some soup that smelled like heaven. I was close enough to hear what the two women at the next table were discussing without being too obvious. I could sense a mix of emotions from them—genuine sadness tinged with the guilty orange sparkle that came with having juicy gossip to share and knowing it wasn't polite.

"...still can't believe they chose Felix over Franz," one was saying in a low voice. "Franz has been teaching informally for years."

"Felix had better people skills," the other replied. "And his work was more... accessible, I suppose. Less intimidating for beginners. And being good in person with witches, is very different from what Felix proposed."

"I know, I was hoping we could tap into the income from plain humans. There are so many more of them, and they love learning how to make things these days."

I tried to look absorbed in my soup while listening more carefully. Here was the lead I needed.

"Well, it doesn't matter now, does it?" the first woman said. "Poor Felix. And poor Tobi. They were so excited about the opportunities it would create."

The second woman sipped her hot chocolate. "Do you think they'll have to cancel the entire program now?"

"We can't. The village needs funds. Maybe Franz can step in after all, though it won't be the same and it will be a while before we can offer classes to plain humans."

They moved on to discussing Christmas Eve dinner plans, but I'd heard enough to realize I'd stumbled onto something important. Some kind of teaching program that Felix had been chosen for, something that involved income significant enough to make a difference to the village.

After I finished eating, I decided it was time to check back in with Klara. She'd mentioned wanting regular updates anyway, and I had questions about these courses.

I found her at the village hall, working through a stack of paperwork. It wasn't only police reports, which made me think about how small communities like this must require people to wear multiple hats, handling everything from law enforcement to municipal administration.

"How's the investigation going?" she asked when I knocked on her open door. "You ready to team up yet?"

"Slowly," I admitted, settling into the chair across from her desk. "But I think I might have found something interesting. I heard someone talking about some kind of teaching program that Felix was involved in. Something about classes online?"

Klara's expression shifted—not quite guarded, but more careful. "No one told you about that? Sorry I thought you knew."

I wasn't sure I believed her. Nothing in her emotions, but she seemed shifty. "No, and it seems like it might be relevant. Can you fill me in?"

She set down her pen and leaned back in her chair. "It's not really a secret, just... well, it's one of those things the village is trying to keep low-key until we're sure it'll work out. It's a bit on the risky side."

I didn't have to ask what kind of risky she meant. The plan to sell courses to plain humans told me everything it needed. I was surprised that the council was willing to try it out. "What kind of teaching are we talking about here?"

"Online craft instruction," Klara said. "Classes for regular people—non-magical folk—who want to learn traditional German crafts. Things like woodcarving, folk painting, bread making, herbal teas, that sort of thing. Felix was chosen to be the primary instructor. We got the idea from watching people do it on social media."

Doing it online was less risky. It was easy to hide where you were filming from and plain human social media was completely separate from the magic one. Felix, or whoever took over now, would need to be careful to keep the instruction away from powers or spells, but scripting would take care of that. I wondered if D would have some ideas.

"That sounds like a wonderful opportunity," I said. "Much broader appeal than magical instruction would have."

"Exactly. The potential student base is enormous, and people are willing to pay good money to learn authentic traditional techniques." She paused. "The plan was also to offer some in-person workshops here in the village—those would be for magical folk, more specialized techniques. But the real income stream would come from the online courses for regular people."

"How did they choose Felix for it?" I asked.

"There was a competition," Klara said, and I sensed she was choosing her words carefully. Her emotions carried a faded scent of roses. It was reluctance, but I couldn't pin down why. "Several people applied. The village council reviewed proposals and made their decision based on teaching ability, communication skills, that sort of thing."

Nothing unusual there. I mean they could filter the people who were simply not capable out at an early stage. "And Felix won?"

"Felix won." She paused, then added, "Though I have to say, it wasn't entirely popular with everyone who applied. Some people felt... overlooked."

Now we were getting somewhere. Was Klara missing out the possible motive on purpose? "How many people applied?"

"Four, initially. Though one of them withdrew her application before the final decision was made." She looked me in the eye like she could read my thoughts—I'd never asked about her powers, so maybe she could. "You think someone killed Felix to get the job?"

"It's the first hint of a motive," I said. "Who are the other candidates?"

Klara hesitated. "I suppose there's no harm in it, since it's common knowledge. Franz Eberl was Felix's main competition—he's been doing informal magical instruction for years. Lotte Dirschl applied too, though her specialty is more in brewing and potions than general instruction. And Konrad Stein threw his hat in the ring, though I think he was more interested in the administrative side of things."

Why was she holding back? "And the person who withdrew?"

"Sabine Kranz. She's the most skilled craftswoman in the village, but..." Klara shrugged. "Let's just say she's not the most social person. Teaching requires patience with students, and Sabine tends to expect people to keep up or get out of her way. No one thought she'd have the right attitude with the plain humans."

I made mental notes about all four names. "How much income are we talking about here? Enough to make a real difference?"

I caught a flash of something deeper from Klara—worry that felt more intense than she was letting on, mixed with embarrassment. The village's financial situation was clearly worse than she wanted to admit.

"Enough that losing the opportunity would hurt," Klara said, and I could hear the understatement in her voice. "The village has been struggling a bit financially—increased costs from suppliers, more expensive magical components for maintaining our protective spells. Felix's teaching program was projected to cover most of the shortfall. The money would go to the village mostly, but whoever did the teaching would get paid."

How could she not think this was a huge pointer to the killer? Germany might have a different culture, but humans are humans regardless of location or magic powers. "That's significant."

"I guess so," she said, chewing her lip. "I should have thought about it. It's not just the money, but what it represents. Felix was going to be showcasing traditional German magical techniques, helping preserve knowledge that might otherwise be lost as older witches pass away."

I could understand why someone might have strong feelings about being passed over for something like that. It wasn't just about the income—it was about recognition, contribution to the community, preserving traditions.

"Where are these other candidates now?" I asked. "Are they all still in the village?"

"Franz and Lotte are here for Christmas, obviously. Konrad too. But Sabine..." Klara frowned. "She went on a retreat right after the decision was announced. Said she needed some time to herself in the mountains. She's not due back until after the holidays."

Was the timing close enough? "How close to Felix's murder was the decision?"

"Look, you don't know the people here, so be careful about leaping to judgment," she said. "The announcement was made before we headed to the market. Sabine left right after. She was in her cabin when it all happened."

Maybe. But in my experience, people didn't always react to disappointment in predictable ways. And a retreat in the mountains was awfully convenient if you wanted to establish an alibi for being somewhere else when Felix died. "Do you think any of the other candidates might have been angry enough about losing to..."

"To commit murder?" Klara shook her head, but I could sense the conflict in her emotions—genuine conviction about her neighbors' character battling with reluctant recognition that desperate situations could change people. "No. Absolutely not. These are people I've known my entire life. Franz might complain loudly about the unfairness of it all, and Lotte might sulk for a while, but kill someone? No."

I could hear the conviction in her voice, but that emotional struggle told me she wasn't as certain as she wanted to sound.

"I'm not suggesting they're bad people," I said gently. "But sometimes good people do terrible things when they're desperate or angry or hurt."

"Not these people," Klara repeated, but the emotions I was reading from her were less firm than her words—doubt creeping in around the edges of her loyalty.

I decided not to push it. Building trust with Klara was more important than winning an argument, especially since I'd only been in the village for one full day. She knew these people; I didn't.

11

After my conversation with Klara about the teaching competition, I decided to go back to chatting with the villagers. I mean, despite a clue, I didn't have any action plan. If I was going to talk to the failed contestants, I needed to know more. Why was I surprised when nobody wanted to talk about murder during the holidays? Not that they actively obstructed me, but it was clear Christmas took priority.

I could understand it, really. Children were running around excited about Christmas morning, families were preparing for evening celebrations, and the entire village had a warm, anticipatory feeling that came with traditions. Murder didn't stand a chance.

By late afternoon, I was feeling more than a little frustration. When I'd come to Germany to fix Felix's spell, I'd thought I'd be home by now, maybe helping with Christmas preparations on Henbane. Instead, I was trying to solve a murder in a community where every normal investigative approach seemed to hit a wall. Mark would have known how to handle uncooperative witnesses. D would have made people feel comfortable opening up.

I was wandering through the village square, feeling increasingly useless, when I spotted Klara coming out of a house. She waved me over, and I felt a bit annoyed—with her or myself, I wasn't sure. Was she investigating without me? What happened to 'we'll work together'?

"Any luck?" she asked as I approached.

"Not really," I admitted. "People are being polite, but nobody wants to discuss anything unpleasant on Christmas Eve. Can't say I blame them."

"Same here," Klara said with a sigh. "I know you thought I was shutting you down, but I want to find the killer. It's just really hard when it's guaranteed to be someone I trust and love." She took a deep breath like she was trying to break the spiral of her thoughts. "I tried to follow up on some details from yesterday, but everyone's focused on family time and celebrations. It feels wrong to push too hard when their friend just died."

Her emotions were in turmoil, professional frustration mixed with genuine respect for the community's need to grieve, all carrying the burned orange reek of stress. But underneath that, there was something else. A hesitation that felt like she was holding something back.

"Maybe we should take a different approach," I said. "Can we sit down somewhere and talk through what we know so far? Pool our information and figure out our next steps?" Yeah, yeah, no new facts, but Klara's mindset seemed to have changed—maybe she'd find a new interpretation of the few clues we had.

"I'm not sure we've learned much more than we knew this morning," Klara said, echoing my thoughts.

"That's exactly why we should review it," I said. "This

morning we were just collecting information. Now maybe we can think about what it all means in terms of the murder. Question any assumptions."

"The cafe is too public," she said, looking over her shoulder at the filled tables inside and out. "My office."

The village hall was quiet, most of the administrative staff having gone home early for the holiday. Klara led me to her small office and closed the door behind us, creating a space that felt cozy and constraining all at the same time.

"So," she said, as she cleared a space on the wall. "What have we actually learned? I'll put it up here to help us see any connections."

I repeated what the animals had told me. The strange scent they'd detected the morning he died, and my theory about using animal witnesses to identify the killer. The fact they knew his emotional state was deteriorating—my interpretation of the squirrel's words. Klara wrote on a stack of sticky notes, placing them on the wall. Then I brought up the teaching competition, hoping her mind was a little more open now.

"Four candidates," I said, counting them off on my fingers. "Franz, Lotte, Konrad, and Sabine. All of them had motive—lost income and public recognition. And Sabine conveniently disappeared on a retreat right after the decision was announced."

Klara was quiet for a moment, and I could sense that internal conflict again—her loyalty to the community warring with her professional obligations. Maybe I was wrong about her changing. I could just push my way through the interviews, but having her there would just make everything easier.

"I keep coming back to the same problem," she said after a few minutes. "I understand why someone from outside the village might see this as a motive for murder. But these aren't strangers we're talking about. These are people I've known my entire life." She wrote the names on notes and placed them on the wall.

"I know it's difficult," I whispered. I've been right where you are. Someone I thought I could trust betrayed everything. "We have to face the reality that whoever killed Felix had access to him over a period of months. That means someone local. The village is too well protected for outsiders to just wander in, commit murder, and wander out again without being noticed."

"How could you understand?" she asked. I saw a flicker of hope that I might be wrong. "You grew up as a plain, right?"

I told her about the cases on Henbane, where I'd had to investigate people I cared about. "So, you see. Finding out someone is capable of murder... it's one of the hardest parts of solving a murder. I'm glad it's not my official job."

Some of the defensive anger faded from her emotions. "Then you know what I mean. Franz has a temper, but he's not cruel. Lotte can be dramatic, but she's genuinely kind. Konrad might hold a grudge, but he's never been violent. And Sabine..." She shrugged. "Sabine might avoid people when she's upset, but killing someone? It doesn't fit."

I nodded, even though I wasn't entirely convinced. "What if we approach it differently? Instead of starting with who could have done it, let's think about the how and when. Maybe that will point us toward answers that feel more... manageable."

Klara looked relieved at the suggestion, her emotions shifting and softening. "What do you mean?"

"Well, we still don't know how Felix died, right? Grete is working on that. And we don't have a precise timeline for when it happened. If we can narrow down those details, it might eliminate some possibilities." And you might be able to accept the truth.

"That makes sense," Klara said. "What else?"

I was about to suggest we think more carefully about Felix's routine and who would have had access to him, when something occurred to me that made my stomach sink.

"Klara," I said, "how well do you know Grete?"

"Grete? Very well. She's been our healer for years, delivered half the babies in the village. Why?"

"She's the one examining Felix's body, determining cause of death. But she also had access to him during his illness. If someone was slowly poisoning him..." I let the implication hang in the air.

Klara's emotions flared and then faded as if she'd put up a shield. "No. Absolutely not. Grete dedicated her life to healing people. She would never harm anyone."

"I'm not saying she did," I said quickly. "But as investigators, we have to consider all possibilities, right? Even the uncomfortable ones?"

"Not this one," Klara said. "There are some people you can eliminate immediately because you know their character. Grete is one of them."

She was determined to convince me, but I also detected something else—a flash of fear that felt more personal than professional. I realized I wasn't just asking her to suspect a respected community member; I was asking her to doubt someone she trusted with her own life, someone the whole village depended on. I waited for her to open up, but this was a closed discussion for now.

"Okay," I said gently. "Let's set that aside for now. What about opportunity? Who had regular access to Felix in the weeks before he died?"

"Well, Tobi obviously. Grete, when she was treating him. The people at the Christmas market where he worked." Klara paused. "Actually, that's most of the village. We're a small community—everyone crosses paths with everyone else regularly."

That wasn't particularly helpful. I was starting to realize just how different this investigation was from my previous cases. On Henbane, I'd had a smaller suspect pool and more obvious motives. Here, I was dealing with a close-knit community where everyone had access to the victim and multiple people had plausible reasons to be upset with him. And maybe the community would rather not deal with a murderer.

The problem wasn't that I didn't know how to investigate murders—I'd proven I could do that. The problem was that my usual approach relied on having my friends and familiar to consult. Everyone here was connected to everyone else in ways that made every step forward a struggle.

"I think we need more information before we can make any actual progress," I said, trying to sound more confident than I felt. "Let's see what Grete learns about the cause of death. That might give us a clearer direction."

Klara nodded, though I could sense she was as frustrated as I was with our lack of leads she could live with.

"Should we try talking to Tobi again?" she asked. "He might be more willing to discuss Felix's routine now that he's had time to process what happened."

"That's a good idea," I said, stifling my urge to tell her we needed to interview actual suspects. "And maybe we can get more details about Felix's interactions with the teaching competition candidates. Even if they're all innocent, they might have noticed something relevant."

As we wrapped up the meeting, I thought that we might

be missing someone important. "What about people who aren't part of the teaching competition?" I asked. "Other villagers who might have had conflicts with Felix that we don't know about yet?"

"I suppose that's possible," Klara said. "But I can't think of anyone who had serious problems with him. Felix was well-liked."

"Still, we should keep that idea open," I said. "Just because the teaching competition seems like an obvious motive doesn't mean it's the only one." And I was going to follow that trail today, no matter what.

12

Tobi was out of the village when we reached out, so we'd catch up to him later. Klara and I parted; she went to search out reports of any problems with Felix and... anyone. I headed out for dinner.

The inn offered roasted pork with red cabbage as a traditional meal, and it tasted like someone's grandmother had perfected the recipe over decades. I finished and was thinking about looking up one of the contestants when Grete approached my table. She looked tired, and her emotions were muted.

"Cossi," she whispered, glancing around the half-empty dining room. "Could we speak privately? I have the results of Felix's examination."

The wonderful dinner turned into a lump in my stomach. "Of course. Should we get Klara?"

"Actually," Grete said, her tone careful in a way that made me pay attention, "I was hoping to speak with you first. As the protector. Not as an investigator. There's a small sitting room upstairs. I think it will be private enough."

The inn's sitting room was cozy in the way only old

European buildings could manage, with thick rugs and furniture that had been comfortable for generations. Like the world hadn't changed since the Middle Ages, when the only sources of heat were a fire and warm blankets. Grete closed the door behind us and took a seat across from me, her medical bag at her feet.

"How bad is it?" I asked.

"Worse than I expected," Grete said. Her emotions were tightly controlled, but I could sense the weight of serious concern underneath. "As we expected, Felix didn't die from natural causes. He was poisoned."

You know when you're expecting bad news, and then you get it. The expecting part doesn't soften the blow. "Are you sure?"

"Completely certain. But that's not the worst part." She opened her bag and pulled out a small vial containing dried herbs. "This is a slow-acting poison. It's been administered over a period of months."

"Months?" Great, the suspect pool was wide open when it should be shrinking. "You mean someone has been systematically poisoning him?"

"That's exactly what I mean." Grete's emotions carried the metallic tang of anger now. "The poisoning was masked by concealment spells designed to hide the symptoms. From the outside, it would have looked like simple fatigue, maybe some exhaustion from overwork."

I thought about what I'd been told about Felix's condition over the past few weeks, how tired he'd seemed, how his magic had been fluctuating. "That's why his enhancement spell went wrong."

"Almost certainly. The poison interferes with magical control. What should have been a simple charm became chaotic because his system was compromised." Grete set the

vial on the table between us. "The final dose was administered within minutes of him dying. Even without the
previous poisoning, that last amount would have been
lethal."

"So someone escalated from making him sick to killing
him." This wasn't someone making a mistake or acting on
impulse.

"That's one interpretation," Grete said. "Another possibility is that the killer miscalculated the dosage. This poison
is tricky—the effective dose varies based on the person's
magical strength and physical condition. Someone who'd
been weakening Felix gradually might not have realized
how little it would take to finish him off."

Okay, so I jumped to the worst assumption. I still didn't
think it was a mistake, but I could hope, right?

"Who would have access to this kind of poison?" I asked.

"That's the problem," Grete said, her emotions shifting
to the pale yellow of uncomfortable admission. "The ingre-
dients are all common medicinal herbs. Any competent
healer or herbalist could brew it. And the spells aren't
advanced—most village witches could manage them."

"So we're looking at someone with medical knowledge
and reasonable magical skills." So, any witch in the world.

"Or someone who had help from a witch with those
qualifications," Grete agreed.

I thought about our conversation earlier, when Klara
had been so adamant about eliminating Grete from consideration. But now I was sitting across from the village's
primary healer, who'd just described a poison that someone
with her exact skills would be capable of creating.

"Grete," I said, choosing my words carefully, "I have to
ask—"

"Whether I could have done this?" she interrupted, her

emotions flashing with an orange spike of pain. "Of course I could have. I have the knowledge, the skills, and the access. Felix trusted me completely—he wouldn't have questioned anything I gave him as treatment. I was treating him, he never balked, no matter what I asked."

"But you didn't do it."

"No." Everything about her told me she was telling the truth, but I didn't have Mark's power, so I could be fooled. "Felix was my patient. I took an oath to help people, not harm them. And honestly, if I'd wanted to kill someone, I'd have chosen a method that couldn't be traced back to me."

She paused, and I could sense a wave of professional guilt swirling around her. "I should have caught this. I've been treating him for months, trying to figure out why his condition wasn't improving. The concealment spells were sophisticated enough that I kept attributing his symptoms to stress and overwork. I feel like I failed him completely."

I believed her—the emotions I saw flowing around her were clear and true. Grete believed what she said. "Who else knew about Felix's condition?" I asked, hoping the answer would give us a suspect.

"Tobi, obviously. He was the one who convinced Felix to come see me in the first place." Grete paused. "Klara knew. She told me about his symptoms weeks before he came for help."

"Klara told you about his illness?" That felt all kinds of intrusive.

"She's responsible for us. She noticed he seemed run down, and knew he'd resist coming to see me—I'll never understand people who think they'll get over something with bothering me." Grete's tone was casual, but I could tell it hurt her that people wouldn't let her help. "You think she did that to point suspicion elsewhere?"

That was the problem with investigating people you knew—every action could be interpreted multiple ways. "No, but I don't have any evidence to clear or accuse anyone."

"I thought that might be the case," she said. "That's why I wanted to tell you in private. You can decide who gets to know the facts."

I didn't really think Klara or Grete were capable of murder, but I could keep her talking. The final lead could come from anywhere. "Who else knew?"

"The village council knew Felix was having health issues, though I didn't share specific details with them. Medical confidentiality still applies in small communities." She sat straighter, as if pulling on a professional cloak. "But they were concerned about whether he'd be able to handle the teaching responsibilities."

If the council knew Felix was struggling with his health, and someone was worried about the teaching program failing...

I really didn't need another pile of motives. What I did need was information about the villagers. "What kind of investigative training does Klara have?" I asked.

"Basic law enforcement, some medical knowledge for handling accidents and injuries." Grete picked up the vial and turned it over in her hands. "I know she checked up on him regularly."

I thought about Klara's reactions during our conversations, the way she'd been so protective of the village's reputation, so reluctant to consider that any of the locals might be capable of murder. She wasn't a suspect, but was she hiding something? "Have you shared this information with anyone else?" I asked.

"Not yet. Like I said, I wanted to get your guidance on

how to proceed." Grete wiped her hands on the side of her pants. "As the protector you're the only other person I'm certain isn't involved."

That was both flattering and terrifying. If Grete was right about the poisoning, then I was on my own in a village where someone had hidden their real self from everyone for their whole life. I guess I had experience with that, too.

"I think," I said, "that we need to be very careful about who we trust from here on out."

"Agreed," Grete said. "What about Klara? Is she part of the trusted group?"

"Yes. She's as determined to solve this as I am." I picked up the vial and examined the dried herbs inside. "Can you think of anyone specific who might have the knowledge to create this?"

"Several people. Lotte brews potions professionally— she'd certainly have the skills. Sabine works with plant materials for her crafts, so she'd know about herbal properties. All the older villagers might have picked up enough traditional knowledge over the years."

"What about the teaching competition candidates?"

"Oh, interesting. Franz doesn't have medical training, but he's lived here his whole life. Traditional knowledge gets passed down in families, but we all share what we know." Grete shrugged. "Konrad has some basic healing skills— nothing formal, but he's helped patch up people after accidents."

So basically, half the village might have created the poison. That wasn't particularly helpful.

"I think we should keep this between the three of us for now," I said. "At least until I can figure out how to investigate without alerting whoever did killed Felix."

"What about the village council?" she asked, frowning as

if it was wrong to question them. "They'll want to know cause of death."

"Can you give them something that acknowledges this is suspicious but doesn't reveal the poisoning details? Maybe that you need more time to determine the exact cause, but that it's clearly not natural death?"

Grete considered this. "I could say that Felix died from complications that require further investigation, and that we're treating it as suspicious pending more analysis. That would keep the investigation going without giving away what we know about the poison."

"Good enough," I said. "That buys us time to figure out our next move."

13

The next morning, I woke to the sound of cheerful voices echoing through the village streets. Christmas Eve had arrived with fresh snow and an excitement that made it feel like the air itself was practically sparkling with anticipation.

It also made investigating a murder feel completely inappropriate. I know Christmas was always going to delay us. But I wanted to be home. I am glad I didn't just turn around after the market situation. Frankly, only because I would have been called back.

I met Klara at the village hall as planned, armed with Grete's official report about Felix's death requiring further investigation. Reluctance flowed around her like a lavender mist. I guess I'm not the only person who wanted to celebrate the season and not reveal the identity of a murderer.

"This feels like the worst time for our investigation," Klara said as she read over Grete's report. "Is it wrong that I was hoping for natural causes?"

"You aren't the only one. I've had overnight to accept

this, but still..." I left off the rest. I couldn't bear to say it with the background of children's laughter echoing from the village square outside.

"It's Christmas Eve," Klara said, making excuses. "People are focused on their families, preparing for celebrations. It feels... intrusive to drag them into police interviews when they're trying to maintain holiday traditions for their children."

I understood the sentiment, but Felix deserved justice, and standing her moaning wasn't going to get the job done. If I was Mrs. V, I'd say that aloud, but I'm not. "I appreciate that it's difficult timing, but we can't let the investigation stall because of the calendar. Whoever killed Felix is still out there. The sooner we find them the quicker the community can start to heal."

"Of course," Klara said, though I caught a flash of frustration. "I just think we might get better cooperation if we wait until after the holiday. But then, there's New Years. I guess it's better to start with a clean slate."

Through the window, I could see a group of kids building an elaborate snow fort in the village square, their parents watching fondly. The scene was peaceful, but that didn't change the fact that someone in this community was a killer.

"We can be sensitive to the holiday while still doing our job," I said. "Maybe we start with informal conversations— checking in on people, seeing how they're doing. Nothing that feels like interrogation, but still gathering information."

Having Klara with me during interviews might limit what information people might share. But it would also give me a chance to observe Klara's reactions and see if I could learn anything about whatever she was hiding.

"That sounds like a good approach," I said. "Should we

start with Tobi? He might be more willing to talk about Felix's last few weeks now that he's had time to process what happened." I mean, a day isn't enough time, but it's all we had.

"Good idea," Klara said, gathering her notebook. "Though we should be prepared for him to be... emotional. He and Felix were very close. I'll bring tissues, and maybe a little calming tea."

We found Tobi at the cottage he'd shared with Felix, packing boxes with Christmas decorations that wouldn't be hung this year. He looked exhausted and hollow-eyed, but when he saw us approaching, I caught a flash of anxious hope.

"Any news?" he asked, inviting us into the cozy front room that still smelled faintly of Felix's woodworking projects. "I don't know what I think you'll tell me, but it's not helping to have so many questions still floating around."

"We only have one answer right now. Grete confirmed that Felix's death is suspicious," I said gently. "We're treating it as crime now."

Tobi's emotions shifted—surprise, then anger, finally settling into entrenched sadness. I'm not sure that solving the case would help him. I'd seen shifters grieving on Henbane. It was powerful, but seemed to fade quickly.

"Good," he said. "Felix didn't just die. Someone did this to him. I was so worried that I missed something. That I could have..."

Klara handed him the packet of tissues and sat. "We need to know everything about his last few days, more if you suspect something."

I appreciated her practical approach. Tobi didn't need someone to cry with him. He needed us to find the killer.

"He was getting better," Tobi said, clutching a tissue.

"Before the Christmas market rush started wearing him down, he'd had a few weeks where he seemed more like his old self. More energy, better mood. He was excited about the teaching program again. Whatever was making him sick, it seemed like he was finally recovering from it."

I exchanged glances with Klara. That could fit with what Grete had told me about the final, lethal dose being administered recently. If Felix had been getting better, someone might have panicked and escalated their poisoning attempts.

"Did he mention anyone he was having problems with?" I asked. "Any conflicts or disagreements?"

"Not really," Tobi said, his emotions spiraling in rays of hope and sadness. "Felix tried to avoid conflict. He was always the peacemaker in any group."

"What about the teaching competition?" Klara asked. "Did he say anything about the other candidates' reactions to his selection?"

Tobi's emotions shifted to something more guarded now. He didn't like to gossip, but it was the only way to help up. "He felt bad about Franz being disappointed. They used to be friends when they were kids, and Felix knew Franz needed the income. But Felix thought the decision was fair —he had more experience with the kind of crafts they wanted to teach online. He didn't feel like he had to apologize for winning."

"Did Franz say anything to Felix about losing?" Klara asked.

"A few things," Tobi admitted, his loyalty clearly warring with his desire to help the investigation. "But Franz complains about everything. It's just his personality. Felix didn't take it seriously."

I didn't want him to think we were targeting anyone specific. Mainly because we were still fishing. "What about anyone else? Lotte, Konrad, Sabine?"

"Lotte was disappointed too, but she handled it better. She even offered to help Felix with some of the herbal components for the craft classes." Tobi paused, looking uncomfortable. "Actually, that's something that bothered Felix a little. She kept offering to bring him special teas and herbal remedies for his fatigue. He appreciated the thought, but he was already working with Grete and told me he didn't want to mix treatments."

My mental alarm bells started ringing. Lotte had been offering Felix herbal remedies, and Grete had found evidence of herbal poisoning.

"Did he ever accept any of Lotte's treatments?" I asked, trying to keep my voice casual. "Before Grete got involved?"

"A few times, early on. But when Grete started treating him more regularly, he told Lotte he needed to stick with professional medical care." Tobi looked uncomfortable with the memory. "She didn't take that well. I think her feelings were hurt."

"How exactly didn't she take it well?" Klara asked, leaning forward with surprise. "I had no idea there was any tension there."

"Oh, she wasn't rude about it or anything," Tobi said. "Just... wounded, I guess. Like Felix was rejecting her personally instead of just being careful about mixing treatments."

If Lotte had been offering Felix herbal treatments and he'd rejected her help in favor of professional medical care, she might have found other ways to administer whatever she thought would help.

When we left Tobi, he seemed a little more settled. It was as if our progress—what little there was—gave him hope. Outside, more families were hanging out, steaming mugs in their hands. Kids building snow forts and parents chatting. Here they seemed to revel in the cold. I preferred Henbane, probably raining, where my friends would join me at Sheena's pub, or Jan's cafe.

"Who else can we talk to?" I asked as we walked back toward the village center.

Klara glanced around at the festive scene. "Maybe we should give people today to focus on their families. Christmas Eve is important here, and one more day won't change anything."

"It's not just one day though, is it?" I said, trying to keep my frustration out of my voice. "Today is Christmas Eve, tomorrow is Christmas Day, and then there's Boxing Day. We're talking about suspending the investigation for three days. Every day we delay gives the killer more time to cover their tracks or destroy evidence, or run."

Klara looked uncomfortable. "I just... I hate the idea of ruining people's Christmas."

"Someone already ruined Felix's Christmas," I pointed out. "And every Christmas he'll have from now on."

But looking at the children playing in the square, listening to families preparing for their Christmas Eve celebrations, I could see Klara's point. "All right," I said reluctantly. "We'll give people Christmas Eve with their families. But tomorrow, Christmas Day or not, we continue the investigation. This can't wait indefinitely, if the we want to solve the murder."

Klara nodded, her relief clear in the way her emotions shifted around her. "That seems fair. People will be more willing to cooperate after they've had time with their children."

"It's not like we're going to interview all these people," I said, waving my arm to encompass the scene. "Just the people who might be killers."

"And might not be," Klara said.

14

Christmas morning in *Sicherheim* was peaceful. After the frustrations of trying to investigate on Christmas Eve, I'd expected to wake up feeling restless and anxious about the delay. Instead, I appreciated the quiet of the village Christmas—the smell of fresh bread and coffee drifting from houses, children's excited voices as they discovered their presents.

It reminded me of Christmas mornings from when I was little, when both my parents were alive and we'd have a quiet family celebration in Vancouver. There was the same sense of warmth and togetherness, the same feeling that this was time set aside for what mattered most.

I was enjoying a lazy morning before Klara and I started working again, when someone knocked on my door. I opened it to find Heinz and Trudi.

"Cossi," Trudi said, "we were wondering if you'd like to come with us to check the crossroads protection. It's become something of a Christmas tradition—making sure every-thing is secure for the coming year. Having a protector with us makes it special."

"Is there some concern about it failing?" I asked, remembering how impressed I'd been with the concealment spell when we'd arrived. Henbane's spell didn't need refreshing as far as I knew, so this was interesting.

Heinz shifted. "Not exactly failing, but... well, with everything that's happened, we want to make sure there are no weak points that might compromise the village's security. And if we're going to be hosting visiting witches for the teaching programs, the concealment spell might need reinforcement to handle the additional magical signatures."

The swirling orange and green emotions told me they were both worried about something more than the spell. "You think Felix's death might be connected to the concealment spell somehow?"

"We don't know," Trudi admitted. "But the spell protects us from outside interference. If someone wanted to harm the village, weakening our defenses would be a logical first step."

They were looking for reasons that the killer wasn't one of the village inhabitants. I couldn't blame them. I would be too if I hadn't been through the same thing so many times. "I'd be happy to take a look. Let me get my coat."

The walk to the crossroads took us back down the winding mountain road I'd traveled with Felix and the others just a few days ago. It felt strange walking the route on foot, seeing the landscape from a different perspective. The concealment spell was even more impressive from this side—I could feel it strengthening as we approached the boundary, layers upon layers of protection built up over centuries. Not even a hint of weakness.

"It's remarkable work," I said as we approached the spot where the road seemed to dead-end against the forest. "The design differs from the concealment spell protecting

Henbane, but just as effective. Whoever created the original spell knew what they were doing."

"The founding families were all skilled in defensive magic," Heinz said with obvious pride. "They had to be, choosing to establish a community in such an isolated location."

"How often do you check on it?"

"Officially, twice a year," Trudi replied. "But some of us come down more often, just to make sure everything feels right."

As we got closer to the concealment barrier, I started noticing local wildlife. A red squirrel watched us from a pine tree, and I could see fresh tracks in the snow from various forest animals. This seemed like an excellent opportunity to get more information about the area's recent activity.

"Do you mind if I take a few minutes to check with the local animals?" I asked. "They sometimes notice things we miss."

Heinz and Trudi exchanged glances. "You mean actually talk to them?" Trudi asked.

"It's one of my abilities," I explained. "Animals see and hear things, especially changes in routine or unfamiliar people in the area."

"That's... brilliant," Heinz said. "I wish we had someone with those powers."

I approached the squirrel, who seemed curious rather than wary. "Good morning. I'm the protector who's been staying in the village. Have you noticed anything unusual around the crossroads recently?"

The squirrel's tail twitched with interest. "I know who you are, protector. Emperor crow told us to help."

Destroyer had no power here because he couldn't fly this

far. Impressive that he held sway. "I'm wondering if you or other animals have seen anything different around this area lately. Any humans who don't belong, any changes to the magical feeling of the place?"

"All the same," the squirrel replied after a moment of consideration. "Not strangers." It paused, head tilted.

"But what?"

"Village witches come lots of times. Smell worry. Always checking. Some argue, some look at spell and leave."

That was interesting. "Arguing?"

"Lots of things. Witches need more money. We don't use money. Food is plenty. Some argue but we don't understand."

I glanced back at Heinz and Trudi, who were examining the concealment spell but leaning toward us. Listening in on my side of the conversation with the squirrel. Two months ago would have been around the time the teaching competition was being decided. Was it coincidence?

It was a long shot since animals rarely recognized individuals, but it wouldn't hurt to ask. "Do you remember who was arguing?"

"Loud-voice he witch, bitter-smell she witch. She very angry, said unfair, said others get chances she never gets." The squirrel's ears flicked forward.

My pulse quickened. "Can you describe the she witch? Hair color, size?"

"Dark-hair, smaller than loud-voice he. Hands smell like plant-magic, earth-magic."

That description could fit several of the people I'd met— Lotte with her potion-making, or possibly some of the other villagers I hadn't met yet. I realized I had no idea what Sabine looked like, since she'd left for her retreat before I arrived.

"Thank you," I said to the squirrel. "This is very helpful."

The squirrel flicked its tail and scampered up the tree, losing interest now that the questioning was over. Since I hadn't set up a payment system, the local animals didn't seem interested—I hoped Destroyer wouldn't send a message about that. I suspected that the witches made sure plenty of nuts and seeds were available.

I rejoined Heinz and Trudi, who had finished their examination of the concealment spell. "How does everything look?" I asked.

"Strong as ever," Heinz said with satisfaction. "Whatever problems the village is facing, the protective barriers aren't one of them."

"That's good news," I said. "Though I did learn something interesting from the local wildlife."

I told them about the argument the squirrel had witnessed two months ago, carefully describing the details without speculating about which villagers might have been involved.

Trudi tried to hide her reaction. She knew the woman. "That timing fits with when the teaching competition was being finalized."

I wasn't planning on letting her off the hook. "Do you know who might have argued near the crossroads around that time?"

Heinz and Trudi exchanged glances. "Could have been several people," Heinz said diplomatically. "The competition brought out potent feelings in some folks."

"What about someone who works with plants and makes crafts? Dark hair, smaller than average?"

"That could describe half the women in the village," Trudi said.

I stopped pressing. Neither of these people was on my

suspect list. If I needed to push them, I'd do it later, with Klara in attendance. The important thing was that I'd learned someone had been angry enough about the teaching competition to have heated arguments about it near the village's protective barriers—more likely they were looking for a private place than something to do with the magic. Combined with what Tobi had told us about Lotte's rejected herbal offerings, I was seeing a pattern that pointed toward specific suspects.

———

15

By Christmas afternoon, the village had settled into a quieter rhythm. The excitement of the morning had given way to contented exhaustion. I hadn't been able to connect with Klara in the afternoon, and I didn't want to bring anyone else into the investigation by asking where I could find the people we needed to interview.

I ate at the inn and then went looking for Klara. I found her at the village hall, where she'd been catching up on paperwork. It occurred to me that she hadn't mentioned any family or friends. She'd been as alone as I was. I should have offered to just hang out with her, but the investigation needed to be finished.

She looked up when I knocked on her office door, her emotions jumping at my presence. I'd have to ask Mrs. V if I should declare my powers when I arrived. It felt sneaky to just read people without giving anyone a chance to shield.

"Ready to start talking to people again?" I asked, not sure what I would do if she said no.

"I suppose we can't put it off any longer," she said, gathering her notebook. "The teaching competition candidates, or have you found more suspects?"

I wish we had one real suspect, but I kept that to myself. "They seem like the logical place to start. Who's most likely to be available tonight?"

"Konrad, probably. He lives alone and doesn't have family celebrations to worry about. Franz might be free too —he's been pretty restless since Felix's death. Sabine isn't back in the village, yet."

So, we started with Konrad Stein, who turned out to live in a neat cottage near the village square. He answered the door promptly—a man in his fifties with a calm, observant manner. Not a twinge of guilt or suspicion in his emotions.

"Cossi, Klara," he said, stepping aside to let us in. "I've been expecting you, of course. Please, sit."

His front room was comfortable but impersonal—the home of someone who spent most of his energy on other people rather than himself.

"Thank you for seeing us," I said, trying and failing to sound less formal. "I know this is a difficult time for the village."

"Felix's death has been... shocking," Konrad agreed. "Though I understand you've determined it wasn't natural causes? Gossip, you know."

I wondered who had shared that information with him —we'd only told the council, and I hadn't expected the news to spread so quickly. Perhaps I should have taken an oath from everyone to keep the news to themselves.

"That's right," Klara said. "Since everyone knows by now, I'll admit we're looking for a killer."

So blunt! I watched Konrad's reaction. He showed appropriate surprise and concern, but underneath I caught something more complex—a thread of what felt like guilty relief, as if some burden had been lifted from his shoulders.

"Can you tell us about your relationship with Felix?" I asked, taking advantage of my status as a stranger.

"We knew each other, of course—small village and all." His emotions carried a tinge of old sadness. "We had a romantic relationship years ago. It ended amicably enough, but things were never quite the same afterward. I doubt that was possible, but it is still a regret. "

That was interesting. I settled back in my chair. "That must have made the teaching competition situation more complicated."

"A bit, yes." Konrad's voice carried rueful humor. "Nothing like competing professionally with your ex-boyfriend. And in front of his current hot shifter husband."

"How did you feel about Felix being chosen for the program?" I asked. I might as well follow Klara's lead and just get to the point.

"Disappointed," Konrad admitted, his emotions shifting to honest frustration. "I thought my experience in mediation and community management would have been valuable for the project. But I understood why they chose Felix—his woodworking was more visually appealing for video instruction. There would be other opportunities. Perhaps a support role for him?"

I found it hard to believe he was so blasé about it. "Weren't you angry about the decision?"

Konrad considered this carefully. "Frustrated, yes. Angry? Not really. I was more concerned about Felix himself."

That held a spark of truth. "What do you mean?"

"He seemed... fragile lately. Overworked, stressed. I worried that taking on such a large project might be too much for him." His emotions carried genuine concern. "I suggested to the council that they might want to have a backup instructor ready, just in case. It is, of course, difficult to make such a recommendation and not sound bitter."

Yep, it could be seen as either considerate planning or subtle undermining of Felix's appointment. I couldn't tell which it was from Konrad's emotional state—he seemed genuinely to have been worried about Felix's health.

"I saw you at the Christmas market a few times, talking with Felix," Klara said. "How did he seem to you those last weeks?"

"I didn't see him much before, but I stopped by his stall at the Christmas market a few times, tried to gauge how he was handling the stress." Konrad was skirting something, but I think it had to do with Tobi not liking their being together. "I'll be honest—I didn't like how Tobi was hovering over him. Felix needed support, not someone treating him like an invalid."

"Did you ever offer Felix any kind of help or treatment for his fatigue?" I asked, thinking about the herbal potion Grete had discovered.

"I suggested he see a proper healer, which he eventually did. Beyond that..." He shrugged. "I'm not a medical person. I tend to stick to what I know."

We talked to him for a few more minutes, but nothing new came up. I didn't think he was our killer.

"It's Christmas, let me pour you a mug of beer," he said when I got up to leave. "You cannot refuse my offer on this day! Oh unless alcohol is... then perhaps a spiced tea?"

Klara accepted before I could say no. He poured beer and told us to return the mugs when we were done. I kind of liked that tradition.

16

Our next stop was Franz Eberl, who lived in a larger house on the outskirts of the village. He answered the door, red-faced and slightly unfocused, with a large glass of red wine in his hand.

"The investigators!" he announced, gesturing us inside with exaggerated courtesy. "Come in, come in. I've been wondering when you'd get around to me."

Franz's emotions were a cheerful muddle I couldn't immediately sort out—excitement, nervousness, and something that felt like relief all swirling together. His house reflected his personality: cluttered, colorful, and overwhelming.

"We're talking to everyone who was involved in the teaching competition," I said, continuing with the direct approach. "Can you tell us how you felt about Felix being chosen?"

"How did I feel?" Franz laughed, settling into an overstuffed chair with his wineglass. "Honestly? Relieved. Do you know how much work that teaching program would have been? Video editing, dealing with student questions, managing the whole online platform..." He took a sip of wine and shook his head. "Felix was welcome to it."

"But you applied for the position," I said, confused.

"Of course I did! Can't let people think I wasn't interested. But between you and me," he leaned forward, "I was secretly hoping they'd choose someone else. Much better to complain about not getting it than actually having to do all that work."

His honesty made me chuckle. His drunkenness removed all shields from his emotions. All clear and mostly happy. There was a little grief at Felix's death. "So you weren't upset about losing?"

"Oh, I was upset," Franz said cheerfully. "But more about the principle of the thing than the actual job. I like to complain—keeps life interesting. Poor Felix got an earful from me about it."

"What did you tell him?" Klara asked, dropping her notebook and pen in her bag.

"That the council preferred pretty faces over real experience," Franz said with a grin. "That his woodcarving was flashy but my techniques had more substance. Felix just smiled and nodded—he was used to my rants."

Franz's emotions shifted to something more sheepish. "We had some conversations about it. I may have been... dramatic about my disappointment. But it was just complaining."

"What kind of conversations?"

"Look, I was upset, all right? I said some things I probably shouldn't have. But it was just talk—I would never have hurt him."

That defensive protest made me more suspicious, not

less. People who were genuinely innocent rarely felt the need to deny harmful intent. "Where were you the night Felix died?" I asked.

Franz's emotions carried a flash of panic before settling into stubborn secrecy. "That's... complicated."

So the jolly drunk was a cover? "How so?"

"I was with someone. Someone who values their privacy. I'd rather not involve them in this unless absolutely necessary."

I let it go for now. "Did you ever offer Felix any kind of help or treatment during his illness?"

"Me? No. I'm not a healer. Though I did suggest he might want to be more careful about who he trusted with his health."

Interesting. "What does that mean?"

Franz's emotions carried spite mixed with satisfaction. "Just that some people offer help for their own reasons. Maybe he should have been more suspicious of people's motives. But I have no details. And I'm sure you're speaking to everyone, so I don't need to name names."

That sounded like he might have been aware of someone else's attempts to "help" Felix—possibly Lotte's herbal remedies. But his emotions read more like he was 'just ranting' again. I hated to think what his online presence might be if he'd been born a plain human.

Our final interview of the evening was with Lotte Dirschl, who lived in a cottage that smelled strongly of herbs and brewing potions. She greeted us with nervous energy, her emotions a swirl of anxiety.

"I heard you're investigating Felix's death as suspicious," she said before we could even settle into chairs. "That's... that's terrible. Who could have done such a thing?"

"We're talking to everyone who knew Felix well," I said. "Can you tell us about your relationship with him?"

Lotte's emotions shifted to painful embarrassment. "We were friends. I... I had hoped we might be more than friends, but Felix was very devoted to Tobi."

This man was like catnip to everyone. "That must have been disappointing."

"It was. But I respected his choice. Felix was always kind about it—he never made me feel foolish or rejected." Her emotions suggested she was being truthful about Felix's kindness, but there was still an undercurrent of hurt and humiliation.

I knew she was hiding something—so many people here were. "How did you feel about losing the teaching competition to him?"

"Disappointed, of course. But not surprised. Felix was the obvious choice for that kind of program." Her emotions carried bitter resignation. "I'm better suited to individual consultations than mass instruction. I offered to share a few recipes with him for teas that plain humans would find useful."

There was my opening. "We understand you offered Felix some herbal treatments for his fatigue," I said, watching for her reaction.

Lotte's emotions spiked with fear. "I'm an earth witch," she blurted. "When I see someone suffering, I naturally want to help."

"Did Felix accept your help?" Klara asked. I was wondering if she planned to let me do all the talking.

"A few times, early on. But then he decided to stick with conventional medical treatment." The hurt in her emotions was sharp and fresh. "He said he didn't want to mix

approaches, which I understood professionally. Personally...
it felt like he was rejecting my expertise."

"That must have been hard to hear," I said.

"Frustrated. Hurt." Lotte fidgeted with a small vial on the
table beside her. "I've been practicing herbal medicine for
almost a hundred years. I know what I'm doing. But Felix
chose to trust a conventional healer over someone who's
known him for years."

"What kind of treatments did you offer him?" Klara
asked.

"Energy tonics, stress relievers, sleep aids. All perfectly
safe, all things I've used successfully with other patients."
Lotte paused, her emotions shifting to something more
defensive. "Everything I gave him was carefully measured
and appropriate for his condition."

That last statement didn't match her emotions. Her
words were confident; her emotions frizzed with fear.

"Did you continue trying to help him even after he chose
to work with Grete exclusively?" I asked.

Lotte's emotions carried a flash of guilt before she got
them under control. "I may have... left some remedies where
he could find them if he wanted them," she admitted, then
added quickly, "Nothing intrusive! Just making help
available."

"Where did you leave these remedies?" Klara asked.

"His workshop, sometimes. The market stall." Lotte
twisted her hands together. "Places where he'd be alone and
could choose whether or not to use them without feeling
pressured. I mean, I didn't want to make things awkward,
but I also couldn't just watch him suffer when I had things
that could help, you know?"

I exchanged glances with Klara. If Lotte had been leaving

herbal preparations for Felix in places where he worked alone, she had ample opportunity to administer whatever she wanted him to have—whether he knew about it or not.

What she described wouldn't kill him, though. And Tobi told us Felix refused to take her treatments when he started with Grete. It felt like I was getting closer, but the final step to catching our killer was still so far away.

17

A fter the interviews with the three competition candidates, Klara and I walked back toward the village center in thoughtful silence. The evening air was crisp and clear, with stars beginning to appear over the snow-covered rooftops.

"So," Klara said, "what do you think?"

"They all had motive and opportunity," I said. "But I can't get a clear read on which of them might have actually done it."

"I was hoping you'd be able to tell if they were lying," Klara said with a sigh. "It's very hard to investigate people you've known for years. Everyone's more complicated than they appear on the surface."

I was about to agree when something occurred to me. "What about the fourth candidate? Sabine Kranz. You mentioned she withdrew from the competition before the final decision."

"She did." Klara's emotions carried a mix of frustration and concern. "And now she's unavailable for questioning until she comes back."

This competition is at the heart of everything. I couldn't get my head around people's reactions. "Tell me more about her. Why would the most skilled crafts person in the village withdraw from a competition she was likely to win?"

Klara was quiet for a moment, considering how much to share. "Sabine is... She's probably the most talented person in the village for traditional crafts. Her woodwork, her textiles, her metalwork—all of it is museum quality. But she's also incredibly private and doesn't suffer fools gladly."

Okay, I didn't know the magical world had museums. "That doesn't sound like someone who'd be intimidated by a teaching competition."

"She wouldn't be. But Sabine has very strong opinions about how things should be done, and she doesn't compromise well." Klara's tone carried fond exasperation. "I think she took one look at the idea of teaching online classes and imagined herself trying to explain basic woodworking techniques to someone who calls a chisel a 'pointy thing' and didn't have a scrap of magic power. The thought probably gave her hives."

Somewhat like my dear mentor. I winced at the idea of Mrs. V doing training. And yet, the image made me laugh at the same time. "So she withdrew rather than risk losing?"

"Or rather than risk having to deal with students who couldn't keep up with her standards." Klara chuckled. "Sabine once told me that the only thing worse than doing something wrong is having to watch someone else do it wrong and not being allowed to fix it. I think she pulled out to avoid winning."

Could we call her back for questioning? "When exactly did she leave for this retreat?" I asked.

"Right after the council announced Felix's selection." Klara didn't look up from the ground as she spoke. "I know how that looks, but Sabine does this sometimes. When village politics or social situations get too complicated for her taste, she just... leaves. Goes up into the mountains until things settle down."

"Can we go to her?"

Klara glanced up at the mountains. "She has a cabin up in the high country, completely off the grid. Uses it when she needs to get away from people and focus on her work."

Okay, it was a long walk. "And where is this cabin?"

Klara hesitated, then smiled. "That's the thing—nobody knows precisely. Sabine is very secretive about her retreat location. She says if people knew where it was, they'd show up asking her to fix their broken furniture or wanting to just chat for a few minutes about craft techniques. According to her, there's no such thing as a few minutes when it comes to people's project problems."

That wasn't helpful in proving her alibi. If no one knew where she was, she could be anywhere.

"When is she expected to return?"

"December 27th. She left word that she'd be back by then for the year-end village meeting."

"That's in two days." I thought about it. "We can't wait that long to talk to her. If she's involved in Felix's death, two more days gives her time to prepare her story or dispose of evidence. Or run."

"I understand your concern," Klara said, "but we can't go searching the mountains for her. The high country is dangerous this time of year, and we don't even know which direction her cabin is in."

"Has anyone ever been to this cabin? Any of her friends or family?"

"Sabine doesn't have friends in the traditional sense. She's cordial with people, but not close. And her family..."

Klara paused. "Her parents died several years ago. She doesn't have siblings. She's pretty much alone in the world, which might be why she values her solitude so much." Klara's voice grew more sympathetic. "Though I think sometimes she's lonely, even if she'd never admit it. She has this habit of lingering at the market just a little too long when people are discussing their projects, like she wants to join in but doesn't quite know how."

I thought about the squirrel's description of the woman who'd been arguing near the crossroads—dark-haired, smaller than average, working with plants.

"What does Sabine look like?" I asked.

"Dark hair, usually pulled back in a practical bun that never seems to have a single hair out of place—I've never figured out how she manages that because it's not a spell. She's not very tall—maybe your height or a bit shorter. Strong hands from all the craft work, and calluses that could sand wood by themselves." Klara's description carried affection despite the humor. "And she has this way of looking at people like she's evaluating whether they're worth her time, though, I think half the time she's just trying to figure out if their project is structurally sound."

That definitely fit the squirrel's description. "Klara, I think we need to try to contact her before the 27th."

"How? She doesn't have phone service up there, no internet. That's the point of her retreats."

"What if we asked the village council? They might have ideas about how to reach her in an emergency."

Klara considered this. "They might. Though they'll want to wait until the 27th rather than disturbing her retreat. The council tends to be protective of people's privacy."

No one seemed to think this matter was urgent. "Even in a murder investigation?"

"Especially in a murder investigation. Nobody wants to believe that someone from the village could have done this."

I could understand that protective instinct, but it was frustrating from an investigative standpoint. Every day we delayed gave a potential killer more time to cover their tracks.

"Let's talk to them anyway," I said. "See what they say about reaching Sabine early."

We found several council members still gathered at the village hall—apparently the evening's interviews had generated enough interest that people were staying late to discuss developments. Matthias Vogel, Trudi, and Heinz sat around the main meeting table with cups of mulled wine.

"Cossi, Klara," Matthias greeted us. "How did the interviews go?"

"Informative," I said diplomatically. "But I have a question about Sabine Kranz. Is there any way to contact her at her retreat? I'd like to speak with her before the 27th."

The three council members exchanged glances. "Sabine specifically requested not to be disturbed," Trudi said. "She uses her retreat time to work on important projects."

"I understand, but this is a murder investigation. We need to talk to everyone who was involved in the teaching competition."

"Sabine wasn't involved," Heinz pointed out. "She withdrew before the final decision."

"Which makes her absence even more suspicious," I said. "From an investigative standpoint, someone who leaves right before a murder and becomes unreachable looks like a suspect waiting for it all to blow over."

Matthias frowned. "You're suggesting Sabine killed Felix over the teaching position? That seems... unlikely. She's not a violent person."

"Neither are most murderers, until they are," I said. "Look, I'm not accusing her of anything. But I need to interview her just like I interviewed the others. It's not fair to eliminate her as a suspect just because she's not here to defend herself."

The council members had another of their silent conversations through meaningful glances. Finally, Matthias spoke.

"We could send someone up to look for her cabin, but it would be dangerous in winter conditions. And there's no guarantee we'd find it."

I was not going to let them put me off.

"An emperor's envoy must get to the bottom of the problem," Destroyer said. "I can send birds to search. You can ask my local subjects." I checked my watch. Yep, late here, early on Henbane. "How long will it take?"

"A day, possibly less if the winds are in our favor."

"I'll let you know. Thanks for chipping in."

"What about magical means? Scrying, tracking spells, anything like that?"

"Sabine is… careful about privacy," Trudi said delicately. "Her retreat location is protected against that kind of detection."

Of course it was. Every lead seemed to hit a wall with the mysterious fourth candidate.

"All right," I said. "We'll wait until the 27th. But I want it clearly stated that this delay is at the council's insistence, not my choice. Please don't delay more than that. I have a home I'd like to get to." Did that sound too harsh?

"It was perfect," Destroyer said. "I must go now."

"We do want this solved quickly, Cossi," Matthias said with a slight smile. "We also have to live with the repercussions. Is there anything else we can help with tonight?"

I almost said to stop dragging their feet, but thought it was a step to far. "Not tonight. But I may have more questions tomorrow, depending on what else I learn."

As Klara and I left the village hall, I thought about the timeline. Sabine had left right after Felix won the teaching position. If she was the killer, she'd had time to set up her poisoning plan before disappearing. The retreat could be a genuine alibi, or it could be the perfect cover for someone who wanted to be somewhere else while their victim died.

Either way, I had no intention of waiting until December 27th to find out which. If the council wouldn't help me locate Sabine, I'd have to find another way to track her down. Destroyer's suggestion would have to wait until morning. The local animals were tucked up in their nests.

18

B y the time I got back to my room in the guesthouse, the combination of Christmas Day festivities and three solid interviews had left me drained. I couldn't turn down the invitations for food and wine— apparently, entertaining the protector was a good luck thing. When I finally shut the room door behind me, I was full of mulled wine and enough *stollen* to feed a small army.

I kicked off my boots and flopped onto the narrow bed, staring at the wooden ceiling beams. On Henbane, I would have called Mark to debrief. Here, with the time difference and my friends scattered across their own holiday obligations, I felt the isolation more keenly than I wanted to admit. And guilt, too—I should have reached out sooner instead of trying to handle everything alone.

Since Destroyer had already talked to me, I didn't need to check the time on Henbane; everyone would be up and doing morning stuff. I propped my laptop on the small desk and opened the video call app, sending invitations to Mark, Lance, D, and Lilibeth. To my surprise, all four faces appeared on screen within minutes.

"Cossi!" Lilibeth's voice came through first, though the audio lagged. "How's Germany? You look tired."

"Gee, thanks for the confidence boost," I said, but I was smiling for the first time all day. "I am tired. It's been a long day of interviews and Christmas celebrations."

Mark leaned closer to his camera, his expression immediately shifting to professional mode. "Do you have a suspect yet?"

"No." I figured news got around Henbane from Destroyer, to Tulip, to Mr. V. "It's complicated."

"It's always complicated," D said. "Is it the holiday? You can just force people to help, you know."

"I know, but it feels like I'm the problem. And there are kids who don't need their Christmas canceled." I'm not sure where this reluctance came from, but maybe I was letting everyone push me around. I just wanted a little certainty before I acted—at least that's what I tell myself.

"You must stop this weak questioning," Destroyer announced. "You are my envoy and cannot make mistakes."

"Thanks," I said, but I wasn't sure what for. I noticed the others looked confused. "Destroyer has checked in."

"Back up," Lance said. "Start from the beginning. What happened to the spell malfunction you went to fix?"

I gave them the abbreviated version: Felix's illness, the poisoning discovery, the village's isolation, and the teaching position competition that seemed to be at the heart of the motive. When I finished, Mark was taking notes, D was shaking his head, Lance looked thoughtful, and Lilibeth was chewing on her lower lip. Great! I had them all worried, and they were too far away to help.

"You're leaving out important details," Destroyer commented. "Like how the local animals were more helpful than the humans. And my suggestions about hoe to solve this murder."

I told him in my mind that we needed to be brief and I'd give him credit later.

"So you have four suspects?" Mark asked. "The competition candidates plus this Sabine?"

"She's the most qualified person in the village for the teaching position, but she didn't even really enter the competition. Everyone says she's gruff and would be abrasive with students, but her craftsmanship is exceptional."

"And where is she now?" Lance asked.

"On some kind of retreat until December 27th. That's the day after tomorrow." I rubbed my temples. "The village council wants to wait until she returns to question her, but I'm not sure that's the right call."

"Why not?" D asked. "If she's been away, she might not have had access to poison Felix."

"That's just it—the poisoning has been going on for months. Someone's been giving him small doses of something that affects his control over his powers. The final lethal dose was recent, but the setup took time."

Lilibeth leaned forward. "What's your gut telling you about the other suspects?"

I considered that. My friends knew I could read emotions, and they'd all had experience with it falling short, or rather my interpretation being wrong.

"Konrad, definitely has some bitter feelings about Felix. They used to be a couple, and he doesn't like Tobi, Felix's partner. But his bitterness feels old, settled. Not fresh and murderous."

"What about the childhood friend turned rival?" Mark asked. "That could be a good motive. We've seen what childhood trauma can do."

"Franz. He's hiding something big, but it felt more like embarrassment than guilt. And Lotte, the woman Felix rejected romantically—she's got some serious emotional intensity around him, but again, it felt more like old pain than recent rage." I was getting a new perspective, but no progress.

Lance nodded. "What about the person who won the runner-up position?"

"Actually seems genuinely nice about losing. I got no negative emotions from them at all." I paused, thinking. "The thing is, none of them felt right for this. The poisoning required patience, planning, and access. Plus, the killer had to know Felix well enough to understand how to affect his magical abilities."

"Which brings us back to the missing person," D said. "This Sabine."

"Exactly. But here's the thing—I feel like I'm moving too slowly. It's been three days since I found the body, and I feel like I'm letting the trail go cold." I thought for a second and added, "I'm not sure how truthful the council is being about her location. It doesn't make sense that no one knows how to find her."

"It sounds fishy to me, but maybe that's normal for the community." Mark's expression grew serious. "Cossi, you're doing fine. Murder investigations take time, especially when you're working alone in an unfamiliar community. Don't let impatience push you into making mistakes."

"Easy for you to say," I muttered. "You're not the one sitting in a German mountain village while a killer walks free." Did I sound as pathetic to them as I did in my own head?

"True," Lance said, "I have an idea that might help with your investigation and your timeline concerns."

This is why I called. Another brain to work on the problem. "I'm ready for any ideas."

"You mentioned the village is protected by a concealment spell at the crossroads, right? What if you asked them to add an alarm component to it? Something that would alert you if anyone enters or leaves the village."

D's face lit up. "That's brilliant. If this Sabine comes back early, or if anyone else tries to flee, you'd know immediately."

"Plus," Lilibeth added, "it would give you some peace of mind. You could focus on gathering information without worrying about suspects disappearing."

I felt some of the tension leave my shoulders. "That's a really good idea. I think Heinz and Trudi would help with that—they're the ones who've been most cooperative with the investigation." And I could talk to my squirrel and fox friends about finding Sabine.

"What about the village council?" Mark asked. "How are they handling having an outsider investigate?"

I grimaced. "Mixed reactions. Some of them seem genuinely helpful. They could send me home, but no one has suggested that. The police officer, Klara, has been professional but not exactly warm. I think It's more like they'd prefer me to do the hard stuff so they don't have to live with it."

"You think they'll leave the punishment to you?" Lance asked. "Wash their hands of the whole thing?"

"I haven't even thought about that,' I said. "And I need to focus on catching the killer first."

"I've been thinking about the next steps," D said. "You don't know if Sabine left on the day she told people. If she hung around she could be the killer. And what if she doesn't return?"

"What do you mean?"

"Well, if she's guilty, she might know people are starting to ask questions and decided to extend her retreat. Or if she's innocent but knows something that could help, she might be scared to come back."

"You humans always assume the worst." Destroyer announced. "You may have all the truth, or not. You cannot know yet. It is good that I sent the message to find her through the birds."

I almost smiled at that. "Destroyer sent a request through the bird network to find her." I'd told him not to bother, but why did I think the Emperor Crow would obey me? "Maybe we'll have an answer tomorrow."

"That's a good backup plan," Mark said. "D's right. You need one for if she doesn't show up as scheduled. Being able to find her and will mean she can't just run."

It was getting late, and my full belly was calling for sleep. "Any more suggestions?"

"I would track her down," Lance said. "You're a protector. You don't need permission."

"I'll talk to the local animals tomorrow to see if they can track her," I said. "Maybe the birds will find her first, or I can speed up the process."

"I think that's a good next step," D said. "The longer this drags on, the harder it becomes to solve. And there's always the risk that if the killer isn't caught, someone else could be in danger. And we want you home."

I ran through some other wild ideas before we ended the call. If only I knew of a spell to drag Sabine in—there wasn't one—or a potion to make people tell me the truth. Okay, there was one of those, but who did I give it to? I had no interest in getting the truth about anything other than the murder.

I had one more call to make, and I didn't want it to be video. I pulled out my phone and dialed Mrs. V's number.

"Cossi," she answered on the first ring. "How are you progressing?"

"Better, thanks to some advice from the team. But I wanted to run something by you. The village council is being cooperative but cautious. I'm worried that if this investigation drags on much longer, the trail will go completely cold. And if the killer isn't caught soon, there's a risk they might strike again."

"Finally showing some sense," Destroyer commented. "About time you asked the proper authority."

"What did you have in mind?" Mrs. V asked, in a change from her usual snapping at me that I should know what to do.

"I'm going to track down my last suspect."

There was a pause, then what sounded almost like approval in Mrs. V's voice. "Indeed. You have full authority as a protector to take whatever steps necessary to expedite this investigation, including pursuing suspects outside the immediate area if required. You are the ultimate authority in this matter. Why do you need me to keep telling you this?"

I felt a rush of gratitude and embarrassment—it was a fair question, and I had no answer. "I don't know. But it's nice to hear it again."

"Cossi." Her voice carried a familiar note of frustration at my lack of confidence. "You are doing well. Trust your instincts and your training. Do not let their discomfort with outside authority undermine your confidence in your own abilities."

After we hung up, I sat in the quiet hotel room for a few minutes, processing the day and the conversation. Tomorrow, I would implement Lance's idea about the crossroads alarm. I would ask the animals to track Sabine's whereabouts because maybe the council didn't know.

19

I woke on Boxing Day feeling more determined than I had since arriving in Germany. The video call had reminded me who I was—not just a guest trying to be polite, but a protector with a job to do. And thanks to Lance's suggestion about the crossroads alarm, I had a clear first task for the morning and a reason to talk to animals.

I pulled on my warmest sweater. The mountain air had a bite to it that reminded me winter wasn't just a pretty backdrop here. Another reason to head home before I ended up borrowing clothes.

The village treated Boxing Day as what they called "resolution day"—a time for making commitments and following through on Christmas promises. It seemed fitting that I was planning to resolve a murder case. Though first, I needed to implement the crossroads spell modification.

I found Heinz and Trudi at the village hall, setting up for some kind of community event. They looked surprised to see me so early.

"Cossi," Trudi said, looking up from arranging chairs. "How can we help you this morning?"

"I want to add an alarm component to the crossroads concealment spell," I said without preamble. "Something that will alert us if anyone enters or leaves the village."

Heinz raised his eyebrows. "That's... quite sophisticated magic. May I ask why?"

"Because I need to know if any of my suspects try to disappear before I can question them properly." I kept my tone friendly but firm.

The two council members exchanged a look, and I sensed their mixture of respect and wariness. They weren't used to outside authority, but they also would not argue with a protector. I must have come across more like Mrs. V than I thought.

"We can do that," Trudi said. "It will take both of us working together, though. And we'll need to modify the existing spell structure carefully to avoid destabilizing it."

At least they weren't resisting. "How long will it take?"

"An hour, maybe two," Heinz replied. "We can start right after the morning community gathering."

That gave me time for my real priority: enlisting local animal help. On Henbane, the animals were practically part of the investigation team. Here, I might have pulled back from bringing them in.

I walked to the edge of the village where the forest began, opening my senses to locate potential allies. The language power made communication possible, but unlike on Henbane, these animals had no particular reason to help me. I'd be more forthcoming with rewards if that's what it took.

My friendly red squirrel chattered at me from a nearby tree, more curious than helpful. "Have you caught the bad witch?"

"Soon, but I need help," I said. "What would I need to pay to get you to track someone?"

The squirrel's tail twitched with what I interpreted as amusement. "Nuts. Many nuts. But I am too small for tracking. You need ground hunters, bigger than me."

Right. I focused my attention lower, searching for larger predators who would have better scent abilities and more reason to pay attention to human activity. "Are any around?"

"Wolves. I will not help with them." She flicked her tail and scurried up the trunk to disappear in the higher branches.

The same fox from my earlier visit appeared from behind a fallen log. She was beautiful—russet coat gleaming in the morning light, intelligent dark eyes studying me with what looked suspiciously like amusement.

"Ah, the human returns," she said, sitting back on her haunches with an air of superiority. "Still struggling with your little mystery, I see. Do you have my eggs?"

"We haven't done our business, yet. I need to confirm our arrangement," I said. "The scent identification plan we discussed before. If I am with the witch who killed you will know."

The fox's tail swished. "You should remember the details. As we agreed, three eggs for my initial cooperation in memorizing the scent at the murder site. Six more if I help you identify your killer."

Wait, that wasn't right. "I thought we said two eggs for the whole thing?"

"My dear human," the fox said with the patience one might show a slow child, "you clearly weren't paying attention during our first conversation. Three eggs to learn the scent, six eggs to identify the killer."

I had the details right, but I guess she was going to renegotiate until the job was complete. "So the scent identification plan, how will that work again?"

The fox sighed dramatically. "As I explained before, humans all smell of strange things—cleaning things, pretty smell things, cooked foods. I can sniff the dead site, and then I can sniff that witch on you. You meet with bad witch. I can tell."

Right, that was brilliant. If I interviewed all my suspects, the fox could tell me which one carried the scent from Felix's murder site.

"When can we do this?" I hoped she'd give me credit for the eggs.

"Tonight, at twilight," she said with exaggerated patience. "Bring the first three eggs to the old oak tree where the human died. I will memorize the scent. Then, tomorrow morning, come back after you have spoken with witches."

I was about to agree when another voice interrupted from ground level.

"I can do it for fewer eggs," a badger grumbled. He appeared from behind a log, looking as grumpy as he sounded.

The fox flicked her tail dismissively. "Badger noses not so good as fox ones."

I didn't want to get involved in a bidding war. The badger might be able to help me with the other project. "Can you find the witch who is outside the village in her cabin?"

"Maybe," he grumbled. "I will need a dozen eggs. I may have to pay others."

The animals learned fast. "Okay, how long do you think it will take?"

"I will know today." He trundled away, muttering about "overcomplicated foxes and chattering humans."

The fox watched him go with obvious disdain. "Badgers," she said, as if that explained everything. "He's been grumpy ever since the first snow. Badgers don't like winter. Are we agreed on our arrangement?"

"Yes," I said. "Twilight tonight at the oak tree, then tomorrow morning after I've interviewed suspects."

"Excellent. I will wait for you tonight, but don't be late. I have hunting to do."

As I walked back toward the village, I felt a familiar surge of optimism. I'd gone from no plan to two pretty good ones. I just hoped that finding Sabine wouldn't turn out to be another dead end.

20

The morning community gathering was breaking up as I returned to the village hall. Heinz and Trudi were waiting for me, along with Erik from the council.

"Ready to modify the concealment spell?" Heinz asked.

"More than ready," I said. "And after that's done, I'll need to arrange interviews with all my remaining suspects. And that includes Sabine. I need to know where she is."

Erik frowned. "Cossi, she specifically said she wouldn't return until the 27th."

Was this a tactic? Have someone new tell me the same 'you have to wait' information so I would give up?

"If Sabine won't come to me, I'll track her down wherever she is," I said. "If you really don't know her location, I have ways to track her down."

Nobody argued, but the emotions flowing from the three people weren't about agreement. They figured I'd give up. Within twenty minutes, we were at the crossroads working on the spell modification. Erik's presence made it go much faster than predicted.

At least now I'd know who came and went. I made arrangements to take the egg payment and spent the rest of Boxing Day trying to make sense of what I knew so far. Klara was absent when I dropped into the town hall to talk.

Back in my hotel room, I pulled out my notebook and started making lists. At the top of the page, I wrote "What I Know For Sure" and stared at the blank space that followed.

Felix had been poisoned over several months. The killer had access to him without raising suspicion and knew enough about magical physiology to affect his spell control. The lethal dose was administered recently.

The motive seemed to center on the teaching competition and the village's need for additional income from online classes. Felix had won the position, which would have provided both prestige and financial benefit.

I started a new section: "Suspects: Maybe."

Under this, I wrote the names of everyone I'd interviewed so far: Konrad, Franz, Lotte, and the runner-up candidate, Heinrich. None of them felt quite right to me. Their emotions were complicated—bitter, embarrassed, disappointed—but not murderously guilty. I wasn't sure this exercise was going to get me anywhere, but there was nothing else to do.

I started another list: "Suspects: Probably Not."

This list was longer and included most of the people I'd met in the village. The families who'd invited me for Christmas dinner seemed genuinely kind. Several council members had alibis or lacked obvious motives. Even Klara, despite her sometimes brusque manner, didn't seem like a killer—just someone who was in over her head with a murder investigation.

The problem? How could I be sure the killer wasn't on my "Probably Not" list? Which meant I was missing something important. I refused to let myself rely on the missing Sabine to be my suspect.

By evening, I was restless and decided to walk through the village to see what was happening. I could hear laughter and conversation coming from various houses. People were making commitments for the new year, sharing stories about Christmas gifts, and generally enjoying continuing the holiday spirit.

I stopped at the bakery, where the owner was chatting with a few neighbors over coffee and leftover stollen. They welcomed me warmly, and I learned more village gossip than I had in all my formal interviews combined.

Apparently, Franz had been acting strange for weeks— not just since Felix's death, but well before. He'd been seen coming and going from the village at odd hours, always looking nervous when anyone asked where he'd been.

Sabine Kranz had been vocal about the teaching competition, calling it a popularity contest and insisting that actual skill should matter more than charm. But she hadn't entered herself, which everyone found puzzling since she was acknowledged as the most technically gifted person in the village. A number of people suggested she would make a good behind-the-scenes expert.

And Lotte had been experimenting with new potion recipes, asking unusual questions about dosages and magical interactions that had nothing to do with her usual work.

All interesting, but still not conclusive. I thanked them for the coffee and stories, then headed toward the forest edge for my appointment with the fox, eggs in hand.

I found her waiting by the old oak tree, exactly as promised. "You are punctual," she said, cracking the first egg. "I appreciate that in humans. Most of your species has no concept of proper timing."

"Can you identify the scent signature from the murder site?" I asked.

The fox finished her egg and moved to investigate the base of the tree where I'd found Felix's body. Her nose worked methodically, and I watched her ears twitch as she processed information.

"Yes," she said finally. "The killer's scent is here, mixed with the death scent and various other humans who have been near this spot since. But I can smell it."

Okay, step one went as expected. "And tomorrow morning?"

"Come back when you have talked to the witches. I will wait for you," she said, starting on her second egg.

I felt a surge of optimism. This was the concrete evidence I needed.

"Thank you," I said. "This could solve the whole case."

The fox paused in her egg consumption to give me a look that was distinctly amused. "Don't thank me yet, human. Wait until you see if you can handle the answer I give you."

Wow, that was so much like Tulip's attitude it gave me shivers.

On the way back to my room, my badger friend stopped me. "You didn't say the birds were looking," he said. "I cannot search too. An eagle said the witch was not in her cabin. You owe me nothing."

He waddled away before I could apologize or ask for details. Sabine's retreat location was still a secret, but she wasn't there. How long had she been gone? Was she ever there?

21

A t six in the morning, insistent knocking on my room door jolted me awake. I stumbled out of bed, pulled on my robe, and opened the door to find a breathless young man I recognized as one of the council assistants.

"Protector," he said, barely pausing for breath. "You need to come. Sabine Kranz has returned to the village."

I blinked, trying to process this through my sleep-fogged brain. "Returned? But she wasn't supposed to be back until tomorrow." And why hadn't I noticed the alarm from the village protection spell? Then my mind took a step out of the confusion. I didn't want to have that alarm going off in my head when I was out of the village.

"She showed up an hour ago, demanding to know why there are rumors about Felix being murdered. She's at the village hall with the council, and she's... well, she's very upset."

"About Felix being dead, or about being considered a suspect?" I asked, reaching for my clothes. Pulled a sweater and sweatpants over my pajamas while I listened.

"Both, I think. Klara is trying to calm her down, but Sabine keeps demanding to speak with the protector immediately." He practically hopped from foot to foot. "Please come."

This changed everything. Instead of interviewing my other suspects first and then meeting the fox to identify the killer's scent, I now had Sabine available for questioning. But I also hadn't had time to speak with the other suspects, which meant the fox's scent test would be less useful. Unless... well, I guess if Sabine killed Felix it wouldn't matter who else I spoke to, would it?

"Where is Klara now?" I asked as we hurried toward the village hall.

"With Sabine. She's been trying to keep her calm while we waited for you."

The boy sped up, and I had to run to keep up. He was scared of Sabine's reaction to being kept waiting—maybe I should be too.

"Can you find Franz and ask him to come to the village hall?" I said. "Tell him I have some follow-up questions about his alibi. And see if Trudi is available as well—I want to double-check some details with her." I added the other suspects to my request, so I didn't have to go searching for people.

The young man nodded and hurried off while I continued toward the village hall. The early morning air was crisp and clear, with the sharp mountain light that made everything look bright.

When I pushed open the hall doors, I could hear raised voices coming from the main meeting room. One voice was definitely Klara's, attempting to sound reasonable and official. The other was female, sharp with anger and genuine distress.

I took a deep breath and headed toward what I hoped would be my final confrontation with a suspect.

"This is ridiculous!" the second voice was saying as I pushed open the doors. "I go away for a few days of peace and quiet, and I come back to find the village full of rumors about murder and investigations and—"

The woman speaking cut herself off when she saw me enter. She was tall and angular, with gray hair that didn't match her smooth skin, pulled back in a bun, and hands that showed the calluses. Her eyes were intelligent and intense, currently fixed on me with an expression that was equal parts fury and curiosity.

"You must be the protector," she said, making it sound like an accusation. "Perhaps you can explain why my cottage was attacked by eagles last night?"

"Cossi Fortuna," I said, extending my hand. "And you're Sabine Kranz?"

She shook my hand briefly—her grip was firm and confident, exactly what I'd expect from someone who worked with her hands. Her emotions were a complicated swirl: genuine shock and grief about Felix, mixed with irritation at being thrust into the middle of village drama, and underneath it all, something that felt like... guilt? Or maybe just the discomfort of someone who preferred solitude being forced into a public situation.

"I want to know what happened to Felix," she said without preamble. "Klara keeps giving me official non-answers, but I need to understand what's really going on here."

"Felix was murdered," I said, observing her reaction. "He was poisoned over a period of several months, with a final lethal dose administered recently."

Sabine's emotions disappeared behind a hard shield as

soon as I told her the news. Her face went white, and I assumed the shield came from shock. Whatever she'd been expecting to hear, it hadn't been that.

"Murdered?" she repeated, sinking into one of the meeting room chairs. "But who would... why would anyone want to hurt Felix?"

"That's what I'm trying to determine," I said, settling across from her. "Which is why I need to ask you some questions."

Klara had been watching this exchange with obvious relief that I was taking charge of the situation. "Should I stay?" she asked.

"Please," I said. "I'd like you here as a witness."

Sabine looked between us with growing wariness. "Am I a suspect? Is that what this is about?"

"Everyone who had contact with Felix is a suspect until I can eliminate them," I said. "Where have you been for the past week?"

"At my cabin in the high country," she said, and I caught a thread of defensiveness in her emotions. "I needed some time away from the village after... after the teaching competition nonsense."

Would I need to talk to animals around her retreat? "Can anyone verify that?"

"I go there specifically to get away from people," Sabine said, a flash of irritation breaking through her emotional block. "The whole point is to be alone. Though I do come back to the village for supplies."

That was interesting—and problematic for her alibi. "How often do you come back?"

"When I need to," she said. "It's not like I keep a schedule."

I sensed she was telling the truth about being at the

cabin, but she looked away when she said it. I might not be able to read her emotions, but her body language was on full display.

"Tell me about the teaching competition," I said. "Why did you withdraw your application?"

"Because I would have been terrible at it," she said bluntly. "I don't have patience for beginners, and I don't like having my work methods questioned or modified for mass appeal. Even I could see how dangerous that would be with plain humans."

"But you were likely to win the position." Okay, not really, but I wanted to hear what she thought.

"Which is why I withdrew." She rubbed her temples. "The village needed someone who could teach, not someone who would scare away students by expecting them to understand complex techniques immediately."

I believed her about that, but the way she refused to make eye contact told me she was hiding something—everyone was here. "Did you have any contact with Felix after the competition results were announced?"

"No," she blurted, then hesitated. "Well, not exactly."

"What does 'not exactly' mean?"

Sabine's face flushed. "I may have... left him a rather harsh note about the competition before I went to the cabin. I was angry about the whole situation, and I said some things I shouldn't have."

Klara leaned forward. "What kind of things?"

"I accused him of winning through popularity rather than skill," Sabine said, her voice small with embarrassment. "I suggested that the village deserved better than pretty woodwork and charming smiles."

That explained the shame I was picking up from her reactions. "When did you leave this note?"

"The day I left for the cabin. So about a week ago."

That timeline might work if she'd made trips back to the village that she wasn't mentioning. The gradual poisoning had been going on for months, and while the last dose had been recent, she could have had opportunities during her supply runs she wasn't being forthcoming about.

"Did Felix respond to your note?" I asked to keep her talking.

"I don't know. I left for the mountains immediately after writing it." She looked genuinely distressed. "Do you think... did what I wrote contribute to what happened to him somehow?"

"I don't think your note killed him," I said. "Felix was being poisoned long before you wrote it."

I noticed she didn't seem entirely convinced that her actions hadn't contributed somehow. There was still that thread of guilt on her face.

"I need to ask where you were on specific dates," I continued, pulling out my notebook. "Can you give me a timeline of when you've been at your cabin versus in the village over the past few months?" I didn't really need that information, but maybe it would put off her defensiveness when we got closer to the murder.

We spent the next twenty minutes going through what she claimed were her whereabouts. Sabine's memory seemed good, probably a result of her attention to detail in her work. But I noticed she was vague about specific dates, and her timeline had convenient gaps that could have allowed for village visits she wasn't mentioning.

When we finished, I wasn't entirely satisfied. Sabine's story was plausible, but there were enough inconsistencies and gaps that I couldn't eliminate her as a suspect. Her emotional responses suggested she was holding something back, though whether that something was murder or just embarrassment about her antisocial behavior, I couldn't be sure. And she had come into the village for supplies within the right time frame.

"I need to speak with Heinrich next," I told Klara as we walked Sabine out of the building. "Can you arrange that?"

"Heinrich?" Sabine paused at the door. "Why do you need to talk to him? He handled losing the competition better than anyone."

"We haven't talked to him yet. I'm being thorough," I said. Now I said it, I wondered why I'd ignored him as a suspect. Also, she didn't need to know I was gathering scents.

It turned out Heinrich was more than willing to speak with us despite the early hour. He was a pleasant man in his forties, with a calm demeanor.

"Terrible business about Felix," he said, inviting us into his neat kitchen and making coffee.

"You don't sound surprised about his death," I said.

"He'd been looking unwell for months," Heinrich said. "Felix was always so vital, so energetic. When someone like that starts declining, it makes you wonder."

I watched his emotions as we talked, looking for any sign of deception or hidden guilt. What I found instead was genuine sadness about Felix's death, combined with relief at having been eliminated from the competition early enough to avoid any suspicion.

"Tell me about the competition process," I said.

"Straightforward enough," Heinrich replied, pouring steaming coffee into mugs. "We each submitted proposals for how we'd structure the classes, what techniques we'd focus on, that sort of thing. The council reviewed everything and made their decision."

"How did you feel about losing?"

Heinrich chuckled. "Honestly? Relieved. Felix was the right choice—he had the personality for teaching, and his woodworking skills were more broadly applicable than my specialty metalwork. I'm much better suited to being the backup option."

His emotions matched his words. No resentment, no jealousy, just honest self-assessment and acceptance— nothing held back or hidden. I was confident Heinrich had nothing to do with Felix's murder.

"Thank you for your time," I said, finishing my coffee. "I appreciate your cooperation."

"Of course. I hope you catch whoever did this."

As we walked back toward the village center, I reviewed my conversations with both Sabine and Heinrich. Heinrich I was confident about—his emotions had been genuine and guilt-free. But Sabine remained an enigma. Her shock about Felix's death seemed real, but there were too many gaps in her story, too many vague responses about her whereabouts.

"Can you arrange for Franz to come in next?" I asked Klara because the assistant seemed to have forgotten my request. "I want to follow up on some things from our previous conversation."

"He should be available," Klara said. "Though he won't be happy about being questioned again."

"Let me worry about that," I said. "After Franz, I'd like to speak with Trudi as well. And then Lotte if she's available."

"That's a lot of interviews for one morning."

"Yes, but we have everyone we need now, and I want to solve this and go home," I said.

22

F ranz arrived at the village hall twenty minutes later, looking distinctly unhappy about being called in for another round of questioning. The village was coming to life now. Children's laughter bubbling up from the square, the soft chime of shop bells, and the normal background noise of life brought me a measure of peace.

Franz's emotions carried a familiar mix of irritation and barely concealed anxiety that I'd noticed during our previous conversation. Being questioned about murder couldn't be pleasant for anyone, especially in a close-knit community like this. Everyone would be happy when this was over and life could begin to heal.

"I don't understand why we need to go through this again," he said without preamble as he settled into the chair across from me. "I already told you everything I know about Felix's death."

"I have some follow-up questions," I said, keeping my tone as gentle as possible, well aware that the outcome of this investigation would point to someone people trusted and loved. "And I need to clarify a few details about your timeline."

Klara placed coffee cups on the table and sat with me. I hadn't thought of making him feel comfortable, and her gesture softened the atmosphere. Franz tasted his drink and nodded.

"Your timeline," I repeated when he took another sip. "You mentioned you hadn't spoken to Felix in months, but several people in the village have mentioned seeing you around at unusual hours. Coming and going from the village when most people wouldn't expect to see you."

Franz's emotional state shifted back to caution. Anxiety spiking into something sharper, more defensive, his body tensed. "I don't know what you mean."

"Franz," I said gently, "I can sense that you're concealing something. It's not necessarily related to Felix's murder, but I need to know what it is. If you have an alibi for the periods in question, now would be the time to share it."

He was quiet for a long moment, his internal conflict playing out across his emotions like a storm front. He turned his coffee cup on the saucer and sighed.

"Fine," he said, his voice tight with embarrassment. "I've been... seeing someone. Someone from the next village over. It's new, and it's complicated, and I didn't want the entire village gossiping about it before I knew if it was going anywhere."

"How long has this been going on?" Klara asked, looking up from her notes.

"About two months," Franz admitted, his face reddening. "Since right after the teaching competition results were announced. I was feeling sorry for myself, and Anna was... understanding."

I felt a wave of sympathy for him. Romance blooming

from a need to be comforted was such a human thing. In a village this small, of course he'd want to keep it private until he was sure it was real.

"Anna?" I asked.

"Anna Blume. She runs the bakery in *Grindelbach*." The flush faded as he spoke. "We met at the regional craft fair in October, started talking regularly, and then when I was feeling low about losing the position to Felix..."

"She invited you to visit," I finished.

"Several times a week," he confirmed. "Usually in the evenings, sometimes overnight. That's why people have been seeing me come and go at odd hours. I've been going the back way, it's only an hour's walk after all, and it saved me from explaining myself to anyone."

Walking an hour each way in this cold? He was smitten. "Can Anna verify your whereabouts on specific dates?" I asked.

"I suppose so, if you really need her to." Franz looked miserable. "Though I'd prefer to keep this between us if possible."

"I understand your desire for privacy," I said, "but this is a murder investigation. I'll need to verify your alibi for at least the most recent time periods."

We spent the next fifteen minutes going through Franz's recent visits to *Grindelbach*. His timeline was detailed and consistent, and more importantly, his alibi covered the period when Felix would have received the final, lethal dose of poison. I had no doubt that Anna would confirm the details.

"Thank you for being honest," I told him as we wrapped up. "I know that wasn't easy."

"Are we done?" he asked.

"For now. I need to follow up with Anna, but I'll be

discreet about it." Maybe his relationship would help him through what was to come.

Franz left, looking both relieved and mortified. He seemed like a decent man who'd just been caught up in unfortunate circumstances.

Klara refilled our coffees. "Can you contact Anna Blume and verify his story?"

"I can call the bakery where she works," Klara said. "But honestly, Franz's explanation makes sense. He's always been private about his personal life, and the timing fits with what people have been observing."

"We still need to check. His timing would be perfect if he made the whole thing up, right? Before you do that, can you ask Trudi to come in? I want to speak with her as well."

Klara raised an eyebrow. "Trudi? She's a council member. Do you really suspect her of murder?"

"I'm covering all my bases," I said. "The killer had to be someone with regular access to Felix and knowledge of magical physiology. Trudi fits that profile."

Twenty minutes later, Trudi Meister arrived looking puzzled but and carrying a plate of homemade cookies. "I thought you might need some sustenance," she said with a warm smile, setting the plate on the table between us. "Long morning of interviews."

It was such a thoughtful gesture that I felt another pang of sympathy for how disruptive this investigation must be for the village. These were good people trying to help solve a tragedy while maintaining their sense of community.

Her emotions carried none of the defensive anxiety I'd sensed from Franz. Instead, she seemed curious about why I wanted to speak with her.

"Cossi," she said, settling into the chair with academic

precision. "Klara said you had some additional questions for me?"

"I'm reviewing everyone who had regular contact with Felix over the past few months," I said. "As a council member and someone with medical knowledge, you would have had opportunities to interact with him."

"Medical knowledge?" Trudi looked confused. "I'm not a healer. My background is in theoretical magical studies, but I wouldn't claim medical expertise. I study all sorts of disciplines."

"But you'd understand how magical physiology works. How someone's abilities could be affected by external influences." I'd been digging into the background of everyone on my list since I started this case, and Trudi was the only one who had such a varied background.

She seemed to read my thoughts, which wasn't possible, right? "Are you asking if I poisoned Felix?"

That made it easier. I didn't have to dance around the topic. "I'm asking about your interactions with him over the past few months."

Trudi's emotions crystallized into something between offense and interest—as if she were both insulted by the suggestion and fascinated by the process. "My interactions with Felix were limited and professional," she said. "As a council member, I participated in the discussions about the teaching program. I reviewed the proposals from all the candidates, including his. After he was selected, I helped coordinate some of the administrative details."

Nothing about his illness? "How often did you meet with him?"

"Perhaps a dozen times over the past few months. Usually brief meetings, twenty or thirty minutes at most. Always in official settings with other council members present." She frowned, digging at some memory. "Oh, I suppose I also met with him about the market. I do that with all our vendors. I was more worried about him this year because he was so tired."

This was a small village where people ran into each other all the time. I still didn't think she murdered Felix, but this all seemed so prepared, like she'd been expecting to be interviewed. I had no interest in digging into petty issues, but I had to be confident that I could cross her off the list. "You didn't talk with him for anything else?"

"I see what you mean," she said, waving her hand as if dismissing something. "We talked all the time about a lot of things. About three weeks ago, he asked to speak with me about some concerns he had regarding the program structure. I admit it went a long way toward us choosing him."

That was interesting. "What kind of concerns?"

"He was worried about maintaining authenticity while making the techniques accessible to plain humans. He wanted advice on how to balance traditional methods with modern teaching approaches." Her emotions carried satisfaction. Trudi enjoyed being consulted as an expert. "It was actually quite a thoughtful conversation. None of the other candidates had asked questions like that."

Nothing about her was hidden—a first for me. "Thank you, Trudi," I said after a few more questions. "I appreciate your cooperation."

"Of course. Though I have to say, this is all rather upsetting. The idea that someone in our village could have murdered Felix..." She shook her head. "I hope you find who did this."

23

It felt like the interviews were a waste of time. I made a few notes, and that process made me see the value of confirming my suspicions. It wasn't the fastest way to solve the case, but eliminating everyone but the killer was progress.

When Klara returned, she had news. "I reached Anna Blume at the bakery in *Grindelbach*," she said. "She confirmed Franz's story. He's been visiting her for the past two months, including overnight stays that cover the time periods we're most concerned about. She said he was in need of a kick in the pants to speed things up romantically, but she was patient."

"Maybe she needs someone who knows him to suggest he commit?" I asked. "It would be nice to think he'll be settled. So, one more interview." I didn't say that's all I needed before I headed to my meeting with the fox.

"Lotte should be here any moment," Klara said, settling back into her chair with her notebook. "Do you think she's the killer?"

"Do you?" I asked. "You know her better than me."

"I'm beginning to feel like I don't know anyone." She rubbed her face in frustration.

While we waited for Lotte, I reflected on how different this investigation felt from my previous cases. On Henbane, I'd been questioning people about their personal business, but there was always an understanding that secrets would be kept within our magical community. Here, I was asking people to betray their neighbors' trust, to consider possibilities that would shatter their sense of safety and community. The weight of that responsibility was heavier than I'd expected. Maybe because on Henbane I would be there afterward to help get things back to normal. Here, I wanted to be gone.

Lotte arrived a few minutes later, slightly out of breath from having hurried over from her herb shop. She smelled of rosemary and chamomile, and her apron had small stains that suggested she'd been in the middle of preparing medicines. Her emotions carried a familiar mixture of nervousness and concern that I'd sensed from her during our previous conversation.

"Cossi, Klara," she said, settling into the chair and immediately reaching for one of Trudi's cookies. "I hope this won't take long. I have a batch of healing salves that need attention, and Mrs. Hoffman is expecting her arthritis remedy this afternoon."

The casual mention of her ongoing care for village members made me hope even more fervently that she wasn't our killer. Communities like this depended on people like Lotte.

"Just a few follow-up questions," I assured her. "I wanted to clarify some details about your recent interactions with Felix."

"I told you before, I offered to help with herbal components for his classes. He was polite about it, but he preferred to work with Grete for any health-related matters."

"I need more details. What exactly were these remedies you were offering?" I asked.

She was quiet for a long moment, her internal conflict visible in the way her emotions shifted and swirled. Finally, she sighed. "They weren't just traditional herbs. I've been working on... enhancement potions. Things to improve focus, boost energy for magical work. I thought if Felix saw how effective they could be, he might want to collaborate on some lessons for the witches who would come to the village."

This is what she'd been hiding? An experiment gone wrong? "Tell me what happened. I can't figure things out if people keep secrets."

"To help people maintain concentration during complex spell work, or recover more quickly from fatigue." She looked embarrassed. "I know it sounds like I was trying to compete with Felix's program, but I thought there might be room for both approaches. I mean, this wasn't for the plain humans. And everything was safe."

"Let me be sure I know what you're saying." I looked at Klara who'd perked up at the confession. She nodded at me to continue. "You gave Felix experimental cures so you could convince him to share the courses with you?"

"All things we've used before. I just combined them differently. I may have... left some samples where he might find them. With notes explaining what they were supposed to do. I thought if he tried them and saw the results, he might reconsider working with me."

Klara spoke before I could. "Did he use them?"

"I thought he had stopped when he started working with Grete. Tobi told me Felix wasn't taking any herbal remedies anymore, that Grete wanted him to avoid mixing treatments." Her emotions were jagged with fear.

I felt a chill. "But what if he lied to Tobi about stopping? What if he continued taking your potions while also taking whatever Grete was giving him?"

Lotte's face went white. "I don't know. If she was prescribing similar treatments... the dosage would be off balance. It could..."

"Could what?" I needed her to tell me the whole truth. This information was the first we'd heard that led to the cause of death. An accident? Please make it a mistake.

"Could reverse the intended effects. Instead of enhancing abilities, the combination might suppress them. Or worse." Her voice was barely a whisper. "Oh gods, do you think Felix was still taking my potions while Grete was treating him? I shouldn't have tempted him."

"You tell me. Were they addictive?" I asked, digging into my memory of illicit drugs. "Would someone continue using them even if they weren't working properly?"

"Not addictive, but... if someone was feeling sick and tired, and they thought the potions might help them feel better, they might keep trying different doses or combinations." She was shaking now. "Especially if they were too proud to admit the remedies weren't working."

"Lotte," I said quietly, "it's possible your enhancement potions may have turned into poisons through drug interactions with Grete's treatment."

Lotte stared at me for a moment, then her face crumpled and tears started flowing. "Oh gods," she whispered. "I killed him. I killed Felix by trying to help him."

"You didn't know," I whispered, reaching across the table to squeeze her hand. "You were trying to help."

"Can I... can I finish my healing salves before you arrest

me?" she asked through her tears, her voice breaking. "There are people in the village who need them, and they'll go bad if I don't complete the process today. Mrs. Hoffman's arthritis gets so much worse in this cold weather, and little Erik has that persistent cough..."

Even in her distress, she was thinking of her community. It broke my heart.

Klara stepped in while I tried to think of an answer. "Lotte, you didn't do anything wrong. Felix chose to mix treatments without telling anyone. That's not your fault."

24

W e convinced Lotte that she wasn't guilty—at least she believed it for now. If this was the answer, Felix had brought it on himself. Why would a witch mess around with medications? We didn't get ill often. Mrs. Hoffman's arthritis told me she must be over two centuries. Bones and joints still wore out, just not as fast as in plain humans. When something was wrong, we listened to our healers. That fact kept me from closing the case.

"So where do we stand?" Klara asked as we sat in her office, sharing the last of Trudi's cookies and watching the late afternoon light slant through the windows.

I reviewed my notes, organizing what I'd learned. "We know the gradual poisoning was accidental—Felix secretly continuing Lotte's enhancement potions while taking Grete's treatment. But someone still delivered that final, lethal dose. Someone who knew he was vulnerable and took advantage of it."

"And that someone was?"

"That's what I need to find out. I need to talk to a fox about a scent."

"I'll believe you, but I'm not sure a fox's testimony will carry much weight with the council." Klara couldn't fully suppress her smile at the thought.

"They won't need to," I said. "They just need to believe me. I'll keep my sources confidential."

Klara offered me a warm coat for my walk to the forest edge. I picked up the eggs I would owe, hoping the price hadn't gone up in the meantime. The evening air was crisp and clean, carrying the scent of wood smoke from various chimneys and the faint sweetness of someone's baking. If it wasn't for the murder, this would be a wonderful place for a vacation.

I found the fox waiting for me at the old oak tree, as promised. She was sitting regally in a patch of snow, her red coat vivid against the white background.

"I was about to leave," she said as I approached. "I did not think you would take all day to visit a few witches."

"I brought your payment," I said, ignoring her comments and setting the basket down within her reach.

She investigated the basket with obvious approval. "Excellent quality. These brown ones are particularly fresh —whoever keeps these chickens feeds them well." She cracked the first egg. "Now then, shall we get to business?"

I shrugged off the coat and held out my arms so she could sniff to her heart's content. "Can you identify the killer's scent among the people I spoke with today?"

The fox paused in her egg consumption and studied me. "Come closer, witch."

I kneeled in the snow, feeling slightly ridiculous but trusting in the fox's abilities. She approached, nose working as she sniffed around me—my hands, my coat, even my hair.

"You've been busy today. I can distinguish several different witch scents, mixed with your own and various other odors—coffee, herbs, wood smoke. You should have focused better."

Great, I'd brought her too much input. "Can you identify the killer?"

"The scent from this murder site is definitely present on you," she said, starting on her second egg. "Fresh contact, within the last several hours. One witch you spoke with today carries the same scent that I detected here when the teaching-human died."

My heart rate picked up. "Which person?"

The fox gave me a look that was distinctly amused. "I can identify scents, not faces or names. I can tell you that the killer's scent is among those you carry, but I cannot point to a specific individual and say 'arrest that one.'"

I felt a moment of disappointment, then realized this was still incredibly valuable information. "But you're certain? A person I interviewed today is definitely the killer?"

"Without question. The scent match is unmistakable." She finished her second egg and looked expectant. "It is old and contains many layers."

I thanked the fox, placed the remaining eggs on the ground, so I could return the basket. I'd stupidly expected a name. I could narrow down the list to old.

The young council assistant who'd woken me at dawn—he'd barely been old enough to shave, let alone plan and execute a months-long poisoning scheme. His emotions had been nothing but nervous energy and the desire to do his job well.

Klara herself? I dismissed that thought almost immediately. She'd been working with me throughout the investigation, showing genuine concern for the village and appropriate emotional responses to everything we'd discovered. Plus, she would have had plenty of opportunities to mislead the investigation if she'd been the killer. And the fox would have smelled her on me earlier.

But what about other people I might have encountered without realizing it? I'd walked through the village several times today, passing people on the street, nodding to shopkeepers, exchanging brief greetings. Could I have unknowingly brushed against the killer during one of those casual interactions?

Back in Klara's office, I spread out my notes and began the process of elimination, but I approached it more cautiously than I'd expected. The warmth of the hall was a welcome contrast to the chilly evening air, and someone had left a pot of coffee brewing that filled the space with comforting aromas.

"The fox confirmed it," I told Klara. "The killer is someone I spoke with today. But we need to be thorough about this."

"Where do we start?"

"The suspects first, Then everyone else if we can't figure it out." I looked at my notes. "Yeah it feels like we're back at step one, right? So, Franz first?"

"We know the last dose was fatal, so the killer had to be here to administer it. Franz has Anna Blume as his alibi for the crucial time periods, which you verified. He was in *Grindelbach* when Felix would have received the final dose." I crossed his name off my list. "His emotional responses were consistent with embarrassment, not guilt about murder."

Klara nodded. "Trudi?"

"Solid alibi too. She was working at the Christmas

market in Dresden with multiple witnesses." Another name crossed off. "And Heinrich seemed genuinely at peace with losing the competition."

"What about Lotte?" Klara's emotions thinned out as she spoke. Regret?

I paused, thinking about her tear-stained face and genuine distress. "Lotte provided the accidental poisoning mechanism, but she had no idea it was happening. Her shock about the drug interactions was completely genuine. Plus, she's been too busy caring for half the village to have time for deliberate murder."

Klara nodded, then looked thoughtful. "So that leaves us with our formal interviews accounted for. But what about other people you might have encountered? You mentioned the possibility of casual contact."

"That's what worries me," I admitted. "I walked through the village several times today, said hello to shopkeepers, nodded to people on the street. What if I picked up the killer's scent during one of those brief interactions?"

"Do you remember anyone specific?"

"Not really. Just the usual polite greetings you exchange in a small village." I stared at my notes, feeling suddenly less certain. "Maybe we're missing something obvious. Maybe there's someone we haven't even considered as a suspect."

"Or maybe," Klara said, "the answer is simpler than we're making it."

I looked up at her. "What do you mean?"

"You eliminated Franz, Trudi, Heinrich, and Lotte based on solid reasoning. That leaves..."

"Sabine," I whispered. How had I forgotten her? "It has to be her, doesn't it? She's the only one without a solid alibi, the only one whose story had significant gaps." I thought about Sabine's emotional responses during our interview.

"She claimed to be shocked about Felix's death, but I'm not sure now, that she let me see her real emotions?"

"You read emotions?" Klara asked, slamming a shield in place. "Could she hide them from you?"

"More possible than I'd like," I said, thinking about cases I couldn't share with her. "There are potions and spells that can create false emotional responses or hide true ones. Someone with Sabine's skills in crafting could create something like that. She's old enough to have learned almost every magical talent."

Klara blew out a breath. "You really think she could do something like that? I would have put money on her being innocent."

"She matches the fox's description. Old and very talented. She had access to Felix through her supply runs back to the village. And she had motive—losing the teaching position that everyone agrees she deserved. If she didn't care about it, why did she leave?"

Klara was quiet for a moment, processing this. "She could have done it. I'm having difficulty believing she would. I guess I just know her too well to question her guilt."

"We need proof," I said. "I can't accuse her on a guess." But even as I said it, I felt a nagging certainty that my instincts were right. Wasn't that what Mrs. V always said? A protector is never wrong.

"There's still something that bothers me," I admitted. "Why would she show up this morning demanding answers? Why not just stay away and let her alibi hold until I gave up?"

"Didn't she mention something about birds driving her from her home?"

"I have once again solved your case," Destroyer announced. "Now you must come home."

"Thanks to my familiar, I think." I stood up, feeling the weight of the conclusion settling over me, but also a lingering reluctance I couldn't quite shake. "I suppose there's only one way to find out for certain."

"And that is?" Klara asked.

"We confront her. But carefully—if she can manipulate her emotions, she's more dangerous than she appears. And she might be using a spell or power to keep us second guessing our facts." I gathered my notes. "And we'll need witnesses. Someone who can verify what she says if we get a confession."

"What about Grete? She should be available." Klara grabbed her phone, ready to call her in.

"Good idea. The more official witnesses we have, the better." I took a deep breath, looking out at the peaceful village one more time. "Time to finish this."

The evening air felt colder as we stepped outside, and the peaceful sounds of village life seemed suddenly fragile, as if the truth I was about to reveal could shatter them.

25

The evening shadows were lengthening across the village square as Klara and I made our way toward Sabine's cottage. The background sounds of the evening contrasted harshly with my conviction that we were about to uproot everything.

"Are you certain about this?" Klara asked for the third time as we approached Sabine's front door. "Once we accuse her, there's no going back."

"The fox was definitive," I said, though I couldn't entirely shake my lingering doubts. "And she's the only one left who fits the evidence."

Klara had arranged for Grete to meet us at Sabine's cottage, both as a witness and because her medical expertise might be needed. I could see the healer approaching from the other direction, her bag in hand and her expression grim.

"You must not be distracted by weaker witches," Destroyer declared.

"Please don't make this harder," I begged him in my mind.

"I will restrict myself to observing if you remain imperial," he said. "Tulip says not to disappoint her."

Great! Now I had two peanut-gallery hecklers. I couldn't shut him off, so I tried to ignore the feeling of being watched.

"I am ready," Grete said as she joined us. "This isn't pleasant, but it was never going to be easy no matter who is guilty."

A satisfied crow grunt sounded in my head.

"Lights are on, and I can smell wood smoke from the chimney," I said. "She's home."

Sabine's cottage was neat and well-maintained, with flower boxes under the windows and a workshop attached to one side. Through the workshop's windows, I could see the silhouettes of various crafting tools and several works in progress. Everything about the place spoke of someone who took pride in their work and their home. Not that I expected murder implements, or bottles labeled poison.

I knocked on the front door. Sabine answered promptly, looking surprised to see the three of us standing on her doorstep. She was wearing a simple work dress with an apron that had sawdust clinging to it, and her hands discolored with what looked like wood stain. I almost missed the shimmer cross her emotions. She was controlling what I saw.

"Cossi, Klara, Grete," she said, wiping her hands on her apron. "This is unexpected. Is everything all right? Did you learn something?"

"We need to speak with you," I said. "May we come in?" I stepped inside without waiting for her to answer—I was all protector now, not a new witch unsure of her position. Destroyer gave me another chirp of approval.

Her front room was as neat and well-crafted as I'd

expected, with handmade furniture that showed both skill and artistry. A fire crackled in the hearth, and the air smelled of wood polish and the lingering scent of honey and wax that she used to finish her work.

"Can I offer you tea?" she asked, though her emotions were shifting toward anxiety, her ability to mask losing strength.

"That won't be necessary," I said. "Sabine, I need to ask you some direct questions about Felix's death."

"I thought we'd already covered that this morning." She settled into a chair across from us, her hands folded in her lap, but I could sense the tension in her posture.

"These are new questions," I said. "We know now that Felix was killed by someone who delivered a final, lethal dose of poison while he was already weakened by accidental drug interactions. Someone who knew he was weakened and took advantage of that vulnerability."

Sabine's face remained carefully neutral, but her emotions were becoming easier to read—layers of guilt and fear pushing through her spell.

"That's terrible," she said. "But I don't understand what this has to do with me."

"Stop wasting time," Destroyer said. "End this now and come home."

"I have evidence that points to you," I said. "I know you've been lying about being in your retreat. I want the truth."

"Just because you can't prove where I was doesn't make me guilty," Sabine replied, and I caught a flash of something sharper in her emotions—not just fear, but anger and defiance.

"You're right," I acknowledged. "Which is why I also

consulted with an animal witness who was present when Felix died. A fox who could identify the killer's scent."

Sabine went still. "A fox? You think vermin will prove I am guilty?"

"She did. The killer's scent was present on me from today's interviews. Someone I spoke with was at the murder site when Felix died."

"And you think that person was me?" Sabine's voice was carefully controlled, but I could sense the emotional storm building underneath.

"I think you delivered the final dose that killed Felix," I said. "And I think you've been carrying the guilt of that action ever since."

For a moment, the room was completely silent except for the crackling of the fire. Sabine stared at me with an expression I couldn't quite read, while Klara and Grete sat tensely, waiting for her response.

"You have no proof," Sabine said.

"I don't need proof in the traditional sense," I replied. "I'm a protector, Sabine. I have certain abilities that allow me to compel truthful answers when necessary."

Her emotional state shifted dramatically at that—fear spiking into something close to panic, mixed with a desperate defiance.

"You can't force me to say anything," she said, but her voice lacked conviction.

"I don't want to force you," I said. "I'd prefer that you tell us the truth willingly. But if necessary, yes, I can compel truthful answers. You know that's part of a protector's ability. The choice is yours."

Sabine was quiet for a long moment, her internal struggle playing out across her emotions like a symphony of guilt, fear, and what felt like relief. I wished I could display them to the witnesses. Finally, she made her decision.

"If I tell you what happened," she said, "what happens to me then?"

"That's not up to me," I said. "The village will decide how to handle justice in this case."

"But you'll make sure they know... you'll make sure they understand why I did it?" Her eyes bored into me. I couldn't imagine what she thought would make a difference.

The words hung in the air between us. Not an admission of guilt, but an acknowledgment of intent.

"Tell us what happened, Sabine," I said. "From the beginning."

She took a shaky breath, her hands twisting in her lap. "I killed him because he didn't deserve what he had. None of it."

Grete opened her medical bag ready to ease whatever Sabine felt. Klara radiated cold fury, her shield forgotten. She felt betrayed and used.

"I'd been watching him for weeks, seeing him get sicker and weaker. I knew about Lotte's potions—I'd seen him collecting them even after he told everyone he'd stopped. And I knew Grete was treating him too." Her voice grew bitter. "He was slowly poisoning himself with his own stupidity, and he still had everything I wanted."

"Arrest her now!" Destroyer shouted. I ignored him.

"So you decided to help the process along?"

"I decided to end it," she corrected. "Felix had what should have been mine—the respect, the teaching position, the community's love. And he was throwing it all away, making himself sick with careless choices."

How had she hidden this bitter soul from everyone? "What did you give him?"

"A concentrated poison of my own making. Something that would interact with the treatments he was already taking and finish what his own poor decisions had started." Her voice was steady now, as if discussing a craft project. "I'm skilled enough to know how magical remedies interact. It wasn't difficult to create something that would be lethal in combination with what he was already taking."

I felt a chill at the calculated nature of her confession. "And you found him under the oak tree?"

"I knew he went there when he felt unwell. I followed him that morning, waited until he was resting against the tree." She wiped her eyes, but her tears seemed more from exhaustion than remorse. "I told him I'd brought something to help with his fatigue. He trusted me—even after the harsh note I'd left him, he still trusted me."

Grete leaned forward and asked. "Why would he take it willingly?"

"I told you he was stupid. He drank it all. Said it tasted better than Lotte's concoctions." A bitter laugh escaped her. "He thanked me for caring about his health."

I needed the whole story. "What happened then?"

"Exactly what I expected. The poison worked quickly once it hit his system. He realized something was wrong, but by then it was too late." Her composure was cracking. "He looked at me with such confusion, such betrayal. He asked me why, and I... I couldn't answer him."

Destroyer told me to execute her, and I continued to ignore him. "But you stayed with him?"

"Until he died, yes. I thought... I thought I owed him that much." The tears were flowing freely now. "He died afraid and in pain, and it was my fault. All of it."

Again, the tears weren't about regret for killing Felix but

for.. I don't know, getting caught? "And then you went to your cabin to establish an alibi."

"I went to my cabin because I couldn't face what I'd done. Every time I closed my eyes, I saw his face. The way he looked at me when he realized I'd poisoned him." She was sobbing now. "I told myself he deserved it, that the village would be better off without someone so careless with his health and his responsibilities. But I couldn't make myself believe it."

She took several deep breaths to compose herself and wiped her eyes on her sleeve. "When I came back this morning and heard people talking about murder, I was terrified that someone had discovered what I'd done."

I didn't believe that at all, but it didn't matter now. We had her confession. I wanted to knowhow she'd fooled me. "Is that why you seemed so shocked when I told you Felix had been poisoned?"

"I was shocked because I thought I'd been more careful. I thought my spell had worked. That I'd convinced you I was genuinely grieving." She looked at me with curiosity. "How did you see through it?"

I studied her. Despite the emotion-masking abilities she'd just admitted to using, her current remorse seemed genuine at first glance. She'd committed deliberate murder, but she was also struggling with the reality of what that meant—not just Felix's death, but her own transformation into someone capable of killing.

"It doesn't matter," I said.

"What happens now?" she asked, looking between the three of us with red-rimmed eyes.

I wanted the answer to that too. I had no idea what the council would do. Neither Klara nor Grete gave me any clues. "The first step will be to tell the village," I said.

26

The confession hung heavy in the air of Sabine's cottage, the crackling fire seeming too cheerful for the gravity of what we'd just heard. "We need to move this to the town hall," I said. "Klara, place Sabine under arrest and take her there. Grete, please go with them, I don't want Sabine trying anything desperate."

"Where are you going?" Klara asked, already reaching for the restraint spells.

"I need to talk to Trudi. We can't just call the council together. I'll tell her the basics so she can prep them. The whole community will need to be informed." I looked at Sabine, who sat slumped in her chair, all the fight seeming to have gone out of her. "This affects everyone."

Sabine looked up at me with hollow eyes. "How long do I have before everyone knows?"

I didn't know the answer, but I was suddenly filled with something I didn't usually feel—confidence. "The council will convene within the hour. After that, it's their decision how to proceed."

She nodded and didn't resist as Klara gave her a weird

version of her rights. Something about an advocate, and a reminder that lying carried its own penalty. The restraint spell drew her hands together in her lap, but there was no other visible clue she was in custody.

I stepped outside into the evening air, pulling out my phone to make the necessary calls. The contrast between the peaceful village scene and the harsh reality of what had just transpired was jarring. Before I could reach out, my familiar reached out.

"Imperially done," Destroyer's voice filled my head, sharp with satisfaction. "There is hope for you as my ambassador. I look forward to further training you in leadership."

"I'm not sure we agree that what you do is leadership," I murmured. "You and Tulip are more alike than I thought."

"I was thinking she'd make a good agent," he said, and I had a vision of him preening at the idea. "Act on my behalf with the protectors."

"I'm not sure she'll agree to be your agent," I said. "More like a *consigliere*."

"She mentioned that," he said. "Perhaps that is a better role. We will discuss it when we are together. This administration of my empire is not as much fun as building it." Despite everything, I felt a smile tugging at my lips. "Any brilliant insights from your imperial perspective?"

Trudi didn't answer, so I called Heinz. "I need an emergency council meeting at the town hall," I told him without preamble.

"What's happened?"

"Sabine has confessed to murdering Felix. The full council needs to hear this officially." No need to waste time softening the blow.

There was a moment of stunned silence. "Are you certain?"

"She gave me a full confession in front of two witnesses. Klara's walking her to the town hall now."

He made a sound like a half growl half sigh. "I'll contact the others. We'll be there as fast as we can. Thirty minutes at most."

While I walked toward the town hall, I thought about what came next. The village square was quiet now, most families settled in for the evening. A few people were out walking their dogs, and several nodded to me politely as they passed. They had no idea that their peaceful community was about to be shattered.

The town hall was already lit up when I arrived, and I could see Klara standing beside Sabine in the corner. Grete was bent over Sabine, holding her wrist and muttering something to her.

"Do not bend to mercy," Destroyer said. "No one will respect you."

"I thought you were too busy to hang around," I said.

"I am never truly gone," he said in only a slightly creepy tone.

"Let me handle this without heckling," I said. "I need to look and sound like a rational person."

He cawed out a laugh and promised to stay silent.

Heinz and Trudi arrived first, their expressions grim and their usual friendly chatter replaced by tense silence. Erik came next, having retrieved Anneliese, who looked shaken from being pulled away from her divination work.

"I've been sensing disturbances all day," Anneliese said without preamble as they approached. "The magical currents around the village have been... wrong. I thought it was just the aftermath of Felix's death, but now I understand there was more darkness here than I realized."

That's the problem with prescience as a power. It was

hard to get concrete details, and no one was willing to believe you until bad things happened.

Matthias arrived last, apologizing for his delay and looking harried. Once all five council members were present, we entered the town hall together.

The main meeting room was set up with chairs arranged in a rough circle. Sabine sat in the center, the restraint spell still active. Klara stood beside her chair, arms crossed and looking ready to drag her off if she made a wrong move. Grete waited outside the circle, clutching her healer's bag.

A shiver went through me. Henbane's council had never been this forbidding.

"Council members," I said, "Sabine Kranz has confessed to the deliberate murder of Felix Reinhardt. She has provided details of how she created a poison designed to interact fatally with his existing medical treatments."

The council members turned away from me as one to stare at her. Their faces showed various degrees of shock, sorrow, and grim determination.

"Is this true, Sabine?" Heinz asked, his entire body wrapped in a mist of shock.

"Yes," she whispered. "I killed Felix because I believed he didn't deserve what he had, and I resented that the village chose him over me for the teaching position. I do not wish to repeat this confession again."

"You have forfeited the right to have your wishes considered. Tell us exactly what happened," Trudi said, her voice steady despite the circumstances.

And so Sabine repeated her confession for the council, describing in calm detail how she had crafted the poison, followed Felix to the oak tree, convinced him to drink it, and watched him die. Her words seemed to thicken the air in the room, making it hard to breathe.

"What do you expect from us now?" Matthias asked. You didn't need my powers to interpret his red face and strangled tone.

"As Trudi so kindly put it, I have no right to expectations," Sabine said. "Whatever punishment means to you. I won't fight it."

I saw her twisted emotions, but the council had no idea how deeply the bitterness went. Sabine couldn't see a future for herself.

Erik leaned forward. "Do you understand what you've done to this community? We've lived in peace here for generations."

"I understand," she said. "I've destroyed that peace. I've made all of you complicit in harboring a murderer."

"We'll need time to deliberate," Heinz said.

"How much time?" I asked. This was the end of my job, right? It felt a bit callous, but I wanted to go home.

"Not long," he said. "This isn't a complicated case—we have a confession and clear evidence of premeditated murder. We need to discuss a suitable punishment."

Anneliese spoke up for the first time. "There will need to be a community meeting. Everyone has a right to know what happened."

"Agreed," Trudi said. "This affects all of us."

I looked around the room at the five council members, each grappling with the reality that their small, peaceful village now had to confront murder and decide how to respond.

"I recommend we convene the community meeting immediately after your deliberation," I said. "Do it tonight, so tomorrow people can start healing."

"Then let's begin," Matthias said grimly. "Send the couriers out to bring the adults to a meeting."

27

The council's deliberation took less than thirty minutes. I know it was their decision, but when Trudi told me to wait in the hallway, I didn't care for it. I was the only person asked to leave, and it felt like they didn't trust me.

"You should not have handed them the power," Destroyer said. "No one tells my ambassador to leave."

"I'm here now," I said. "How bad can it be?"

"I understand humans used to punish a thief by cutting off a hand," he said. "Are you happy if they use that logic?"

I wasn't, but I still thought they should make the decision. "I can always change it," I said. "I am the protector. What would you do if this was a crow?"

"We act swiftly and decisively."

When Heinz opened the door and beckoned me back into the main room, the council members' faces were grim but resolute. They'd reached a decision.

"We're ready to convene the community meeting," Heinz announced. "In the larger hall."

I watched through the windows as families walked up

the path together, neighbors stopped to exchange worried words, and elderly residents were helped along by younger villagers. The entire community was coming together, drawn by the unusual nature of an emergency evening meeting.

"No kids?" I asked Klara who'd joined me.

"They will be safe at home. Parents will choose how to deliver the news."

The main hall filled rapidly. I estimated that over a hundred people had gathered. There would be questions and objections and demands of proof. We'd be lucky to finish by New Year's Day. My fingers itched to start checking flights, but I didn't pick up my phone.

Heinz called for attention, and the room fell silent.

"Friends and neighbors," he began, his voice carrying the weight of his years as a council leader. "We've called this emergency meeting to inform you of developments in Felix Reinhardt's death. As you know, we've been investigating the circumstances, and tonight we have answers."

He looked around the room, making eye contact with various community members. "I'm going to ask Cossi Fortuna, the protector who conducted this investigation, to explain what we've learned."

I stood up, feeling the weight of all those eyes focused on me. These people had welcomed me into their homes, shared their Christmas celebrations with me, and treated me with kindness and respect. Now I had to shatter their sense of safety and community trust.

"I came to your village to experience a local Christmas. Instead, I found Felix under a tree. My mission from that moment has been to find his killer."

"And you think I'm pompous!" Destroyer said, breaking his promise of silence.

I paused as a ripple of shocked murmurs ran through the crowd. Several people looked around nervously, as if trying to identify who among them could do such a thing. I realized Sabine was under a conceal spell.

I continued when people settled. "Felix Reinhardt was poisoned by someone he trusted, someone who knew about his medical treatments and deliberately created a substance that would interact fatally with his existing conditions."

A few people rubbed charms, but I held everyone's attention.

"That person," I continued, "has confessed to the crime and provided a full account of how and why she committed murder."

"Get it over with!" Destroyer said.

"Sabine Kranz poisoned Felix because she resented his success and believed she deserved the teaching position that the community awarded to him."

The silence that followed was deafening. Then, as the reality sank in, the hall erupted. Voices raised in shock, denial, anger, and grief. Several people turned to stare at Sabine, who sat with her head bowed, not meeting anyone's eyes.

"That's impossible!" someone shouted from the back.

"Sabine wouldn't hurt anyone!" called another voice.

"She's been part of this community for her whole life!"

Heinz stood and raised his hand for silence. It took several minutes for the crowd to settle enough for him to speak.

"Sabine has provided a full confession," he said. "She has admitted to creating a poison designed to kill Felix by interacting with his medical treatments. She followed him to the oak tree, convinced him to drink the poison, and watched him die."

The second wave of reaction was different—deeper, more personal. This wasn't abstract shock anymore, but the genuine grief and betrayal of people who had known and trusted Sabine.

"Why?" someone called out. "Why would she do such a thing?"

I looked at Sabine. The conceal spell lifted, and the villagers fell silent.

Sabine looked around the room, defiance in her eyes. Now there was no turning back. "Because I was jealous," she said, her voice carrying over the crowd. "Because I thought Felix didn't deserve what he had, and I couldn't stand watching him have the life I wanted."

"So you killed him?" The voice belonged to Tobi, Felix's partner, who had been sitting quietly in the front row. His face was streaked with tears, but his voice was steady. "You killed the kindest man in this village because you were jealous?"

"Yes," Sabine said.

The admission hit the crowd like a physical blow. The reality of betrayal from within their own community was almost too much to process.

Matthias stood up. "The council has deliberated on appropriate punishment for this crime. Given the severity of Sabine's actions and the threat she represents to community safety since she shows no remorse, we have decided on the following measures."

This was it. My question was about to be answered. How far would this council go?

"Sabine Kranz will be stripped of all magical abilities permanently," Matthias announced. "Her memory will be altered to remove all knowledge of magic and this community. She will be relocated to Dresden with a new identity and background that explains her skills as an artisan. The community will provide six months of financial support to help her establish a new life."

I felt the world tilt for a second. Strip her magic? That was far harsher than I'd expected from this gentle community. Removing someone's magical abilities entirely was one of the most severe punishments possible—changing the fundamental nature of who they were.

"She will have no memory of any of us," Trudi added. "No ability to return here or cause further harm. She'll live out her life as a plain human, able to practice her crafts but unaware of the magical world she's leaving behind."

No one objected. This serene little village was okay with this extreme reaction. I glanced at Sabine. She was staring at the floor, but her shield had shattered. Still no regret.

"When will we be free of this... aberration?" someone asked.

"Tonight," Erik said. "The spells required are complex and will take several hours to complete. By morning, Sabine will be ready for relocation to her new life."

"Harsh but speedy," Destroyer said. "You are not happy? Why are you not demanding they obey what you wish?"

"I don't know what's fair here," I admitted to him. "I have no alternative to offer. If they don't have a prison, or don't know they can send her away, what can I do?"

His caw definitely sounded like he'd lost patience with me. The fact he left reinforced my interpretation. Not that he ever really left me, but there was definitely a space between us. Good, no more interruptions and maybe I'd find another solution.

"How do we move beyond this?" Konrad asked.

Had I missed the opportunity to alter this outcome?

Heinz looked around the room thoughtfully. "We heal

by remembering that one person's terrible choices don't define the rest of us. We've lived in peace for generations, and we'll continue to do so. But we'll also remember that trust must be earned and maintained, not assumed. This punishment was in our charter. We have never used it until today. I hope this is the only time we do."

The meeting wound down soon after Heinz spoke. I was deeply shaken by the evening's events. Not just the murder confession, but the community's response to it. The punishment they'd chosen was both more creative and more severe than anything I'd encountered in my previous cases. Heinz announcing this wasn't just made up on the spot didn't make me any more comfortable. A punishment created in the time when witches were being burned—not that many, most victims were plain human women—was too harsh for current times.

"Let it go," Destroyer said. "You knew this might happen, remember Vancouver's council. You cannot fix this incident, learn and grow. You are part of the empire."

"Fine, but this needs to stop," I said, not quite sure what I meant by 'this'.

"Perhaps this is a mercy," he said. "She will forget the pain that caused her to act. She will start a new life."

28

I didn't sleep well that night. Every time I closed my eyes, I thought about what was happening in the council chambers—the complex magical work required to strip someone of their abilities and rewrite their memories. By dawn, I'd given up on rest and was sitting by my room window with a cup of coffee, watching the village wake up to its first morning without Sabine Kranz.

The silence in my head felt strange after days of Destroyer's commentary, but the time difference meant he'd be deep in sleep now. I was truly on my own to process what I'd witnessed.

I couldn't shake my discomfort at the severity of the punishment. I'd seen exile, imprisonment, even magically enforced community service in other cases. But the complete erasure of someone's magical identity felt like something more than justice—it felt like creating an entirely new person. I'd wanted that to happen to me all the time when I was a kid. Mostly the normal wanting to be 'the one' of all teenagers. But now? Was is because my parents suppressed my magic? Would Sabine miss what she didn't have, or would she even know that something was gone?

A knock at my door interrupted my thoughts. I welcomed the break in the spiral of pity I'd fallen into. I opened it to find Klara, looking as tired as I felt.

"The council's finished," she said without preamble. "They want to transport Sabine to Dresden immediately, and they've asked if you'll accompany us."

Not sure why, but this was my opportunity to get out, so I didn't ask. I stuffed my belongings into my carry-on bag as fast as I could. "How is she?"

"Different." Klara's expression was hard to read. "The memory alteration worked completely. She doesn't remember any of us, doesn't understand why she's here, and keeps asking about getting back to work on some furniture orders she thinks she has waiting."

So no longing for something she doesn't know she's missing. Maybe I was overreacting—read that as making it all about me. "She doesn't remember the murder?"

"She doesn't remember magic exists. As far as she knows, she's always been a plain artisan who specializes in traditional German woodworking and textile work. The council created a complete background for her—she thinks she's been living in a small workshop outside Munich and came to Dresden to explore new markets for her work."

"What about her personality? Is she still... her?"

"I don't know how to answer that," Klara said, rubbing her eyes. "Did we really know her before? I guess she seems lighter somehow. Not happy, but not carrying the weight of bitterness and resentment we saw yesterday."

We walked together toward the town hall, my case making tracks in the snow, where I could see a small group gathered around what looked like a modest sedan. As we got closer, I recognized several council members speaking quietly with a woman I barely recognized as Sabine.

The transformation was startling. She stood differently —more open, less defensive. Her face, while showing natural concern about being in an unfamiliar place, lacked the hard edges of resentment I'd grown accustomed to seeing. When she spoke to Trudi, her voice was polite and genuinely confused rather than sharp or dismissive.

"Excuse me," she said as we approached, "but I'm afraid there's been some mistake. I was told someone would help me find accommodation in Dresden, but I don't understand why these people keep acting like they know me."

Trudi looked at me with an expression that mixed relief and sadness. "Sabine, this is Cossi. She's going to help escort you to Dresden."

"Oh, wonderful!" Sabine's face lit up with a genuine smile I'd never seen from her before. "I'm Sabine Kranz. I do traditional crafts—woodworking, weaving, some metal-work. I've been hoping to find new markets in the city."

The name was the same, and the face was familiar, but everything else about her had changed. The bitter, isolated woman who had murdered Felix out of jealousy was gone, replaced by someone who seemed almost... pleasant.

"It's nice to meet you," I managed, shaking her hand. Her grip was firm and friendly.

Heinz approached with a folder of documents and drew me aside. "Everything's arranged," he said. "The apartment in Dresden is ready, six months of expenses are covered, and all her identification reflects her new background. She has samples of her work to show potential clients, and letters of introduction to several craft shops that are expecting her."

"Am I supposed to bring her up to date?"

He smiled. "You didn't like our decision. I wanted you to see that we haven't dumped her."

"This is very generous," Sabine said, looking through the folder. "Though I have to admit, I'm not sure how I got here or why I can't remember traveling to this village. Everything feels a bit... foggy."

"You've been working very hard," Trudi said gently. "Sometimes when artisans focus intensely on their craft, they can lose track of time and details. The important thing is that you're here now, ready for a new opportunity. This is only what we agreed to pay you for the workshops."

"The disorientation will fade after she gets a good night's sleep," Heinz said quietly to me. "Memory alteration needs time to fully settle. By tomorrow morning, her new background will feel completely natural to her."

Sabine accepted this explanation with the trust of someone who had no reason to doubt the kindness of strangers. It was heartbreaking and disturbing in equal measure.

The drive to Dresden took about two hours. I sat in the front passenger seat while Klara drove, with Sabine settled comfortably in the back, occasionally commenting on the scenery or asking polite questions about Dresden's craft markets. Her conversation was light, pleasant, and normal—nothing like the sharp, defensive woman I'd interrogated just yesterday.

Whatever else I might think about the ethics of it, the council had given her a life free from the jealousy and resentment that had consumed her before.

"Tell me about your work," I said, turning to engage Sabine in conversation.

Her face brightened. "Oh, I love what I do! Traditional German techniques passed down through generations. My woodworking focuses on furniture pieces that blend function with artistry—tables that tell stories through their grain, chairs that fit perfectly in mountain homes." She gestured enthusiastically. "And my textile work draws on old patterns but adapts them for modern needs."

She spoke with passion and expertise, but also with a lightness that had been absent from her previous personality. This woman didn't seem the type to go off on a solitary retreat.

"Do you have family?" Klara asked from the driver's seat.

"Not really," Sabine replied without apparent sadness. "I've always been focused on my work. I suppose that's why I never settled down anywhere long-term. But I'm excited about Dresden. I think it could be a good place to establish myself more permanently."

The apartment the council had arranged turned out to be a pleasant one-bedroom space in a building that catered to artists and craftspeople. It was furnished simply but comfortably, with good light for detailed work and space for Sabine to set up a small workshop area.

"This is perfect!" Sabine exclaimed, exploring the space with obvious delight. "And you said the rent is covered for six months? That's incredibly generous. I don't understand what I did to deserve such kindness from strangers."

Klara helped Sabine settle in, showing her where everything was and providing contact information for the craft shops that were expecting her. Throughout the process, Sabine radiated gratefulness, enthusiasm, and ease with her new situation.

"I should let you get settled," I said finally, feeling like I was witnessing something I wasn't sure I should be part of.

"Thank you so much for your help," Sabine said, giving

me a warm hug that startled me with its genuine affection. "I hope we meet again sometime."

I checked my phone for flight information. I'd been able to book a departure for later that evening, giving me time to help settle Sabine but not adding another night away from home. After days of this emotionally draining investigation, I was ready to return to Henbane.

"Airport?" Klara asked, starting the car.

"Please. My flight leaves at eight."

When we reached Dresden Airport, I thanked Klara for her help throughout the investigation.

"Will the village be all right?" I asked as we said goodbye.

"We've survived worse things than this over the centuries. We'll adapt, learn, and continue. We always do."

hree days later, I was back on Henbane, sitting in Mrs. V's kitchen while she prepared what she called thinking tea. I could hear the wind making the pines whisper in her yard, and the background noise of Tulip and Destroyer bickering. I was wrapped up in the warm blanket of home.

"You didn't make much of a mess of your first solo case?" Mrs. V said, settling into her chair with her own cup of tea. "What have you learned?"

She'd actually given me a couple of days to recover and process. I should have a clear answer, but of course I didn't have one. "It was... complicated," I said. She already knew the overview but hadn't commented on her views. So, I gave her all the deets and feels. Maybe she'd have some wisdom to pass on.

Mrs. V listened without interruption, occasionally making notes in a new notebook. This one was titled, *Bigger Issues*.

"Did I handle it correctly?" I asked. "Should I have intervened when they decided on memory alteration? Should I have questioned their justice system more? Should I have started with that? I mean it would still have found the killer, so knowing the punishment wouldn't make a difference, right?" What happened to the confidence I felt in the village?

"Stop questioning everything at once," Destroyer said. "A wise ambassador listens."

"Destroyer is correct," Mrs. V said. And I swore that I'd find a way to cut the pipeline that ran from my mind through Destroyer to Tulip to Mrs. V.

She broke into a smile for a split second, and I knew that had made its way to her too. "You followed your instincts," Mrs. V said. "You investigated thoroughly, identified the killer. We have no way to enforce rules about punishment, and each community lives with different threats from plain humans. Your desire for perfect solutions will always be frustrated."

It felt, as usual, like I'd been rebuked. I thought about the words. She was completely right, but the situation was completely wrong. "We can't let it be anarchy."

"Different communities handle justice differently," Mrs. V replied. "Your discomfort with their methods is under-standable, but not grounds for interference. Not until we have more protectors."

Sure, we could wait around for the universe or whatever to assign more protectors, but that was going to take generations.

"Why do you refuse to speak that aloud?" Mrs. V asked. "You are well aware I hear everything you think eventually."

"Fine, maybe that's how I can stop them telling on me all the time." I glared at Tulip, who was lounging in the corner. "What bothers me most is that I don't know if what they did was justice or just convenient. They eliminated a problem and gave everyone a clean slate. The punishment was listed in some old charter and hasn't been updated since...I don't know when."

Mrs. V nodded. "Those are reasonable concerns. We cannot go back and change what happened. We must move forward."

"I suppose," I said, still feeling uncertain.

"Your job was to investigate and solve the case," Mrs. V said, her tone becoming warmer. "Which you did. What happened after was village business, not protector business. At least for now."

"So what's next?" I asked. "More research? More spell practice? Another crisis to solve?"

"Something you learned is pertinent," Mrs. V said.

She stared at me as if I'd suddenly realize what she meant. It just made me more nervous. I really needed to deal with this reaction. I stopped freaking out and ran everything through my memory. It wasn't the case, nor the first problem at the market. Destroyer told me he knew but wouldn't tell me because I wasn't a fledgling. I kept going until I reached the list of people I'd met. Klara!

"Not everyone doing a job has the normal powers?" Why did I make that a question?

"The protector shortage," Mrs. V said simply. "The committee has solved our first problem, so I can assign them the biggest threat."

I looked confused. "They solved the social media post problem?"

"Marcus came up with an answer. It passed a field test, I'm told. He developed a spell that makes cameras capture what people expect to see rather than what's actually there. He said something about a filter. I didn't need the details. No more blurring effects that draw attention—now when plain humans take photos at magical events, they see exactly what they think they should see."

"That's... that's huge," I said, understanding the implications. Plain humans accidentally photographing magic had been one of the committee's biggest ongoing challenges, especially with AI getting better at spotting anomalies in images. "And he's just a kid."

"Indeed." Mrs. V studied me. "Your experience with Klara may be a solution, at least, in the short term."

This didn't require any thought. "Training witches to handle certain protector responsibilities. We could do it here. Use The Inner Spell. When do we start? How do we start?"

"Good to see you excited," Mrs. V said. "We are in for a busy time. Tomorrow, we start a new year and a new project."

"Can't we start today?" I had about a thousand ideas spinning around, and Destroyer was squawking about being dizzy.

"Tomorrow, more auspicious." She cleared the tea things into the sink. "Today you should enjoy the celebrations to end the old year. Think carefully about your wish."

The wish was a tradition my parents kept going in Vancouver. No magic involved, but still much better than a list of resolutions waiting to be broken. "Are you going to party?"

"In my own way with my friends."

I took that as my cue to leave. The party was about to start, anyway. I ran home and changed into a long peasant dress and sneakers and grabbed my raincoat just in case. D and Mark were waiting on the street when I ran out. We grabbed our bikes—I'd really missed Beulah—and headed for Sheena's.

The shifter bar was full of hot-looking people—I wondered not for the first time if there were ever just normal-looking shifters, or was the gorgeousness just a side effect. Lance headed over with beers for all of us. "Let's sit outside. No need to waste the heating spell."

The evening was the most fun I'd ever had at a New Year's party. None of the frantic need to have fun that plain humans carried with them. Just booze, dancing, food, games, all fun all the time.

D danced with me, hugging me in tight and giving me a kiss. Mark stepped up for the next one and spun me around until I was doubled over in laughter. His kiss was quick and in the shadow, like we were stealing a moment. I loved both of these men, and I didn't think I could ever choose. On Henbane, that was fine. It was going to take me a lot longer to be comfortable with it.

Eventually, pre-dawn bleached out the stars, and it was time to wish. I stood with my pen in hand looking at the slip of paper I'd throw in when I was ready. The others scribbled a few words and ran to the flames. Lilibeth stared hard at what she'd written before marching up to toss it high—she told me she wished the same every year. A familiar.

I wrote my wish for the year. Something that could happen right away because in a few hours I'd be back with Mrs. V.

Make me confident so I can protect our world.

WANT MORE?

~

Cossi leaps into another challenge. Who knew teaching
witches to be protectors would be so deadly?
Use the QR code to grab your copy of A Cursed Course.

~

REVIEW REQUEST

~

If you enjoyed reading A Strange Spell, please consider helping other readers to find the story by using the QR code to leave a review.

FREE BOOK

Use the QR code to Claim your copy of Magic Will Out when you sign up for my newsletter and follow Cossi as she seeks answers to her past.

ALSO BY POPPY

For more books by Poppy Bridgeman

scan the QR code below.

ABOUT POPPY BRIDGEMAN

Hi, I'm Poppy Bridgeman, the cozy mystery alter ego of Canadian author P A Wilson. Poppy was "born" because sometimes stories need a gentler touch—with a little magic, a dash of humor, and plenty of sleuthing spirit.

As Poppy, I write the *Witch of Henbane Island* series (where witches and festivals collide with mysteries), the *EB Eats Culinary Mysteries* (a small-town diner, a determined heroine, and murder on the menu), and the *Pages & Paws Bookstore Mysteries* (a Devon bookshop, two mischievous corgis, and plenty of secrets tucked between the shelves).

When I'm not tangled in my characters' escapades, I'm happily tangled in yarn—I knit, weave, and doodle in sketchbooks between writing sessions. I also love to travel, finding inspiration for charming settings, quirky characters, and suspicious strangers wherever I go.

Home base is the Vancouver area, where I juggle writing as both Poppy and P A Wilson. Whichever name is on the cover, I'm always chasing the next story.

 X

ACKNOWLEDGMENTS

Writing may look like a solitary pursuit, but I could never do this alone. I've been lucky to have support, encouragement, and inspiration from so many corners that it's impossible to thank everyone properly—but I'll try.

My writing groups keep me sharp and creative: The Vancouver Writers Social Group challenges me to see stories in new ways, The Royal City Literary Arts Society has given me the chance to learn from generous and talented writers, and The Other 11 Months group reminds me that words on the page are what really matter. My critique partners, with their sharp eyes and honest feedback, make sure each story is the best version it can be.

And of course, my heartfelt thanks to my beta readers. You catch the wobbly bits, cheer for the good ones, and remind me that these stories aren't just mine—they're meant for you, my readers.